Plantation America

Plantation America

"I Pledge Allegiance to Africa America and to the Republic for which our Nation stand under God and Liberty and Justice and Freedom for all Humankind for we are all United as One."

Sgt. Wayne A. Pope Sr.

PLANTATION AMERICA

iUniverse books may be ordered through booksellers or by contacting:

iUniverse
1663 Liberty Drive
Bloomington, IN 47403
www.iuniverse.com
1-800-Authors (1-800-288-4677)

ISBN: 978-1-4917-4950-0 (sc)
ISBN: 978-1-4917-4949-4 (e)

Library of Congress Control Number: 2014922407

Printed in the United States of America.

iUniverse rev. date: 01/19/2015

Contents

✝ *Rest in Peace* Dedication ✝

God knew you before your Birth…May he know you by his
side in the Afterlife for we are all his Children's

My Prayer to All Gods Children's

My' Dad…Jake William Pope…May your Soul R.I.P

My' Mom…Pearl Rose Robinson…May your Soul R.I.P

My' Grand Mother and Father…May your Souls R.I.P

My' Step Dad…Carlee Peeples…May your Soul R.I.P

My' Aunties n Uncles n Cousin's…May your Souls R.I.P

All my Fallen Soldiers and Friends…Rest In Peace

Special Dedication

Mrs. George' Annie Kay Richardson

Mrs. Ron 'Linda Faye Adam

Mrs. Charles Yolanda Pope…Lt. Charles. A. Pope…USMC

Ms. Jackie Eileen Pope

Mr. William Jake Pope

Mrs. Carl' Wendy Renae Dixon……..Cpl. Carl …USMC

Mrs. Jerry Allen Tamika Davenport…R.I.P Jerry Allen Pope

…………My favorite Cousin…Lupe May Wilburn…………………

Extra Special Dedication
"For all those that ever fought against Racism of the World."

My Children's
Prince n Princess

Lacreashia Shantel Pope...U.S. Navy

Wayne Anthony Pope Sr....U.S. Army

Monique Nicole Pope

Nicholas Cole Pope

Zavion Armad Pope

Ayla Amaya Pope

Jonathan Joshua Pope

Grace Tyra Booth Pope

Hope and Dreams

I dedicate this Book to all our Hopes and Dreams of becoming something greater than what we are today for each Birth that comes into this World is Special. Our inner ability is a result of what gave us Life from the beginning as we carry DNA of our Ancestry forward into a New Generation of Births. God gives us our first breath into his World of Life and Liberty and with Liberty comes ability to live your Life to your fullest. Loves each day as if tomorrow doesn't exist and each other as if it was your own blood. We are all Special in this World that we must all share until we depart our physical existence into the next form of Life...May the Creator of all Life bless each and every Soul and our Love Ones that are no longer with us...God Bless the World and Keep us Healthy until he bring us Home to be joined with his Children's that was here before Us.

Wayne A. Pope Sr.

This Novel follows Devils Angels Gods Children a mystical World Wide Seller of a New Earth Born Species that not just effect man but the entire world. We have no choice but to accept a New Creation greater than us or be wipe out by a greater Predator that birth like an uncontrollable Disease. It's been Rated 5 Stars. In which Devil Angels is been followed By Resurrection, this book is destined to become one of the great books of all times for this normal man who walks beside us is the Resurrected One, his ability is equal to Jesus Christ himself but what he brings into this world is nothing compared to what he leaves behind. The entire World will never sleep the same again in the comfort of their Homes. It also follows Woman Scorned Wendy's Revenge…when enough is enough and there is nothing left but the hidden demonic bloodline to fight with as it take her boyfriend in a world of lust betrayal and never ending terror that get the entire world attention in the worst way. He is left with a lifetime of never ending change in the worst ways known to man.

The Soldier is soon to be released.

Chapter 1

Mayor Office

The sound of me opening the door that needed repairs due to the heavy squeakiness while looking at the most important man known to us. He glanced.

"I thought I told you to get that fix and it been several days now and that noise is driven me crazy every time that door open."

"Mayor, I'll get it fix today but we've a much more important matter that you must look into like now mayor." I said

The sight of him taking what I had to give him displayed his frustration.

"Like what is now, more housing better job, less taxes or better education system needed?" Mayor ask.

"No Mayor, none off that for now." "Maybe later sir."

The sound of me laughing afterward wasn't what he wanted to hear.

"The governor of this state want to meet with you regarding that ignorant rich little kid, did you read this Mayor?" I ask.

"Yes I did!" He replied aggressive like.

"Mayor, my opinion." "I think we should just let this one go and released the Whitfield kid sir." I said.

I knew it was something that he has heard repeatedly by so many as he stood there moving papers around looking down at his desk while glancing up at me in silence.

"It's been almost a month now right?"

"Yes, Mayor about 4 week now sir." I said mildly.

"About that!" "Why can't those uppity politician understand that I didn't have anything to do with that young kid breaking the law?" 'He is no different from anyone else who breaks our rules and regulation that we must all live by don't you think?" This is our country the mayor shouted!"

He was right but this little bastard wasn't like anyone else, he was pull out a different crouch than me or the Mayor and that alone make him different.

"Mayor, I understand that sir, but this kid isn't like the rest of the inmates we've in our custody, he happen to be one of the richest young bastards in America!" I said.

"His family is rich!" 'He is nothing no more than a spoil kid who thinks he can do whatever he wants and when he wants, because of his family!" 'Maybe in America but this is our country, not his family" 'this young man is going to get what is coming to him and like I'm telling you as anyone else." 'I'm not stopping nothing, it will only send out a powerful message that we are to be respected if not for who we are, than the laws we up hold!" Mayor said loudly.

"Ok but you are up for re-election Mayor and we've to input our best interest on the decision you're making sir." I responded concernly.

"Look, he will get his punishment just like everyone else who breaks our rules and regulation and my decision should have no effect on me being reelected!" look at what I have done and the industry that I've brought to this city, this community respect me for what I have done and if they voted for me once, they will do it again young man." Mayor yell after slamming his hand down on his desk.

This man had so much hot air from one word to the next.

"And upon that note, Mr. Pope...his family can take him back home after he clears our medical examination of release" 'In fact let me ask you something Mr. Pope."

"Yes' Mayor." I responded.

"Do we've over crowed prisons?"

"No, Mayor." I responded.

"Do we've a high crime rate?"

"No Mayor." I responded.

"Do you think this little spoiled bastard once he is releases, do you think he will ever come back to the City of Liberation and break our rules and regulations or our laws?"

"No Mayor."

"Then this matter is solved as far as I'm concern alone with this conversation." Mayor said.

"Ok, Mayor." I responded

I watched him walk around knowing he was done with his hot air.

"Mr. don't just say ok to agree with me because it makes me think that you're weak and if we're to make this work, I need your strong opinion. It one of the many reasons I like who you're but you know my punishment work.

"Yes Mayor, you're very effective." I responded none aggressively.

I watched him stand there looking at me when silence had come between us, it made me forget why I had come in here to begin with. I was just about to leave.

"Oh, Mayor!" 'I'm sorry sir but the Governor still wants to meet with you sir."

"The, Governor of Liberation?" He responded looking nervous while sipping his morning sugar with a little coffee added.

"Yes, Mayor…that's the one sir." I responded quickly.

The sight of him standing there looking confuse only told me that no matter how strong minded he was, he still had to face someone higher than him. I watched him intake more air after he leaned over his desk fumbling around with some scatter papers before looking back up at me.

"Ok…well have my secretary to set up the meeting on your way out for the following day around early morning and I want you there as well…meaning no disappearing acts on this one Mr."

I was just about to leave when I had been stopped.

"Hey, I want you there, do you understand me?"

"Yes, Mayor." 'I'll keep the entire day open sir."

"Good day." Mayor said.

"Thank you Mayor." I responded.

Chapter 2

Ms. Glasco

I'll never understand why he had this thing for mid-evil literature artifacts and novels that he enjoy reading back to back, especially the punishment that existed in those dark times. Maybe that why he acts the way he does, his own insanity was his problem in my eyes, this man was a political barbarian by nature I truly believe. But he was the boss around here, I was nothing more than his assistance, it was my job to be his voice, therefore I could only hope that my opinion actually matter to him. One day when this little incident was all said and done the only thing I knew is that nothing good was going to come from it.

Because this was getting completely out of hand and right about now I needed a pick me up of any kind knowing the mayor was going to make my hair as grey as his before I find myself in the seat that he sits before my time. I found myself in the cafeteria thinking I needed another cup of coffee would do the trick but the sight of several new interns must to have found their way into the house of drama. They truly was a sight but I had to see how the booties look, it tell so much about a woman and all I could say is that dam. Those girl look like some good eating all day and night knowing whomever they were dating, they can't be staving or hungry or at least I wouldn't be.

"I see you are busy at work as always." It was Ms. Glasco, the b*tch of b*tches.

I knew there was no one in the area when I took it upon myself to see those jiggly fountains of youth but she must too appear from the darkness like a bat or something.

"Oh, how're you Ms. Glasco." I replied after taking my eyes of the booties.

"Not as good as you it appears." She said oddly.

"Um, what can I do for you Ms. Glasco?" 'Those interns. Well I thought, there was something that I needed to say to them but I couldn't remember what it was as I look at her looking at me like if I was some kind of pervert or something.

"Really." 'It look different from where I'm standing." Ms. Glasco said looking down at me.

"Um, you know that I'm second in charge, right!" I said.

"Yes, im aware of your title Pope." Ms. Glasco said loudly.

"Well, you know that you don't have to call me by my last name, this is not the high school football team or the hood." 'I the second in charge around here and maybe that should come with some respect, wouldn't you agree Ms. Glasco!" I told her loudly.

"Ok, Pope."

I watch her look around several times all serious, this woman knew nothing about smiling what so ever.

"Anyway, I'm glad I found you Pope." 'This is about the improvement for the playground in Paradise Town Center that you've be fight breathing down my neck about.

"Ok." I replied walking away.

"Pope, I need you to sign these now because you tend to have this habit of vanishing without warning. Ms. Glasco said loudly.

I had been so excited about this project from the begging and now with my signature it, this show was about to be on the road. Everyone fought me on this project and how they say that it wasn't needed to upgrade that area. I was told by many that it was nothing more than a reason for the city to be sold from the first serious accident. They were right, the area had become heavily infected with traffic once the mayor decided to create more stores that now surround the once quiet park.

Most of the time they talked about parking and the homeless that seem to having taking haven but all I wanted to do was give the kids a better area to play while there parent wine dine or shopped. We both ended up going deeper inside the cafeteria and all I truly wanted to do was sighed this and get out of her sight. The sooner was the better as we both taking seats after we gotten what we wanted to snack on, this woman had so many document to be signed. It was a lot for a few part toys. I listen to her express her negative commit and her view of high blood pressure among us and how I really needed to eat healthier.

I had taking another sip after telling her to live a little knowing her husband was not hitting her right. Stubby peoples can't handle a woman with all that longness and big breatasis.

"Mr. Pope, hey I'm up here." She shouted loudly.

"Sorry, Ms. Glasco, I was just admiring your pendant, um' is that antique silver?" I asked.

I found myself apologizing when she pushed my hand away from her chest area like if I was trying to get a free touch of the boobies.

"I just wanted to feel history, it been around a while right?" I ask

"It belong to my mother before she passed away." She said.

Ms. Glasco was a cougar for sure with those full lips and cat eyes and darkest chocolate skin, it was plain as day why her midget of a husband married her.

"You know, you look very attractive for a woman your age." I said.

She said nothing back but I knew her little old short man probably baby that thang, she need someone like me who would put it to the test.

"I need you to concentrate on these papers." Ms. Glasco said.

She explained how she could go over each one but there was no need for that none sense knowing that these papers has been reviewed. If I would've listen to her, this woman would've me here for more than an hour easily while noticing other signatures as well. The sight of her alone was making me wonder if the creases in her dress was cause by big bloody granny panties or silky sexy ones trapping the 60 inch plus ass and hips of her. Her lawyer looking dress attire was doing nothing for all the woman hood that she was bless with from birth. I was just happy to see her walk away but I had turned away when she turned around.

"Oh by the way, did you've anything you wanted to ask me concerning these documents?" Ms. Glasco ask.

Chapter 3

Joy

There was nothing for me to say but no while watching that booty jiggling in all directions until it was out of my sight.

"God the creator in heaven knows that her midget of a husband wasn't serving that correctly but to each...its own I guess."

I sat here a few more minutes before going back to the espresso machine to refill before leaving, I had taking the loose change from the collection basket. It wasn't hurting anyone but I had been surprise by someone appearing from thin air.

"Hey, how are you...you know this crappy coffee is to dam expensive. I said.

"Um, um, um I fine sir, how are you." 'I'm, Joy Mayor!' 'I'm sorry sir, I mean Mr. Pope!" She said loudly.

"Hey, calm down we're all family here and I'm not the Mayor, im his assistance, the number two man but if something happen to him then I'll be." As I laugh.

I stood there watching her but not once did she laugh, it had taking her a moment to figure out that I was only joking and nothing more. This woman had no sense of humor but her little young body was banging and probably not ran up in that much.

"Sorry sir." She replied once more.

"Well, I see that you've a lot of you mind Ms. Joy.

She stood there looking at me funny, it made me wonder if she saw what I had done only seconds ago.

"So, how're you Ms. Joy right…you know I was just making change seconds ago."

She stood there looking into the basket, we both saw that it was completely empty.

"I see sir." Joy said softly.

Second of silent had come between us while she look at me puzzled, it was like if she knew me in the worst way or something. Girls her age is nothing but trouble from beginning to end as I tried to say her name again.

"It's, Joy. She shouted loudly.

The thought of someone watching her outburst caused me to look around, this place was nothing more than drama waiting to end your career.

"Ok, is there anything I can do for you Joy?"

She wanted more for the way she was looking at me insanely.

"Sir, really!" She shouted loudly again.

"Excuse me um Joy right." I said.

"Dammit!" 'Really, you don't remember me?"

I looked at her once again and nothing had come to mind while looking around to see who was watching her loud blackness.

"Sir, you spoke at my graduation class in Dallas and when I finally gotten you to myself, there was so many questions I had concerning my degree that I need answer and all I gotten from you and I quote sir your exact words was that, it not what you know to get into this prestige world but it who you know."

"And?" I ask.

"Sir you said you would put in a good word for me."

She stood there looking at me crazy.

"Well joy, is anything wrong, you seem bothered about?" I ask.

"Sir, you can't be that ignorant!"

"Joy, that enough of this your disrespecting me, your days maybe shorten if she don't control that mouth of yours" it want be tolerated in this places place business especially in my presence because I'm your boss and you're not mines.

"We had a sexual relationship and you talk me into getting our baby aborted…you paid for it, remember.

"Hey calm down woman, you're making a scene." I told her.

"It really is true about how much of a bastard you really are, you impregnate that many women that you can't even remember!" 'Go to hell!"

I watched her jiggle away name calling me but that ass was shaking like San Francisco and not once did she look back. My head felt like it wanted to explode any, that young girl got some deep inner issues and how could I not remember hitting something that. She must have me confuse with someone else noticing several peoples were looking our way. I had done nothing but politely waved saying by.

Chapter 4

Cousin

"Hey."

The sound of someone yelling like they back on the block.

"Oh, shit!" I said.

I watched him get closer as I turned around, it wasn't the n*gga I needed to see right now but then again, I knew I would've to deal with him sooner or later. This was the type of n*gga that always had something going on from one day to the next. He was the type that you didn't want as a neighbor or even living in your neighborhood and that was for your own safety.

"Hey cousin." He shouted while bumping into me like we back on the block as we both stood there after I pushed him back saying this is how civilized peoples do it.

I wanted to ask him one simple question before another word came from that mouth that was a storage place for foul disrespecting words.

"Hey are you the janitor or what Mr. Bowen?"

"Cousin what are you talking about." He replied after looking around.

It alone made me wonder about what he has done lately while his hands fumbling around with his pants like if he was searching for something. His commits was inappropriate, especially around women passing by looking at him.

"Mr. Bowen, really." I said.

*"These b*tches know they be wanting the big d*ck!" 'That why these hoes up hea be looking at this big budge, these hoes be knowing whatz real cousin."*

He eventually remove his hand from his crotch area while crossing his arms across his chest defensively like if he could care less about what I had to say from this point on.

"Mr. Bowen, are you the janitor or what, if I remember I put in good word just to get you in here and it wasn't easy at all." 'There was no money to hire another but I made it happen for you cousin."

He stood there looking at me as I waited to see what was going to come from that mouth of his, you never *know about this n*gga.*

"First!" you didn't do shit but set a hard working ole man up to get fired, oh yea...a n*gga heard the really story behind closed doors, it even sadden my heart to hear of such talk and I know something about who you really are cousin!" 'You may have these idiots fool but I'm your blood and you remember that cousin, today and tomorrow." Mr. Bowen said.

"Cousin you talk a lot, but like I ask you one simple easy question and you give me an unwritten book." 'Are you the janitor or what?" It's a simple answer." 'Are you or not?" I ask.

"Yea!" 'Why you ask if you already know the answer. Mr. Bowen said hostilely.

My cousin was a handful and more.

"Mr. Bowen, ok now that we've that under control, now did I ask you to personally take a look at the mayor door or not?" I ask.

He stood there looking at me like if I was stupid or something until I threw my hands up while waiting for his answer. Sstoppped

"Yea, you did." He said aggressively.

"So why haven't you done it yet Mr. Bowen?" I ask.

"Hey cousin, why you got to be calling me Mr. Bowen, we family right." He responded while smirking from ocean to ocean like if this was a joke or something".

"Mr. Bowen, do you like working here or what?" I ask.

"What that supposed to mean?"

"Mr. Bowen, the mayor wanted you personally to repair his door. I said.

"Why me, the man don't like nothing about me, you tell Mr. Shit Don't Stink to fix his own dam door and when did you become his spoke person, you his little erring boy now or do both of you doing something on the down low."

"Listen hear Mr. Bowen, don't fight me…just do it please." I yell.

I left walking away listening to him yelling none stop.

"First you ain't my boss and don't play me like one of your little ass kissing doughboy around here, I don't have yur education or your political career but let's not forget why you even exist here cousin and most of all why I'm I really here." Mr. Bowen yell.

He stood there looking at me stop dead in my track before I return trying to shut his big mouth but he just whispered in my ear while other had taking notice of us.

"Before you get all big headed cousin, you remembered what I done for you or should I shout it out to all your nosey as co-workers right here and now.

I stood slightly back looking at him, this n*gga was too smart for his own good.

"You tell that bastard of a boss of your that he can shove that door up his old fat hairy grey ass for all I care."

I watch him walk away yelling 15 years as loud as he could, there wasn't much else for me to from that point on.

"Hey, I'll let the lead janitor know about what we just talked about and it shouldn't take no more than 15 minute I shouted while he was walking away.

I had to throw something in there to throw everyone off, my cousin was a walking time bomb waiting to explode any second.

Chapter 5

Office Drama

It was less than an hour of making my rounds of this place, the sight of my bar looked pretty tempting and it wasn't even lunch time yet. It was so tempting but a small brandy and coke was just what I needed after dealing with my uncontrollable cousin, that n*gga had my blood pressure almost record breaking and even worse. He knew that there was nothing I could even do to him but I had no one to blame but myself I guess.

"Wow, already!"

There wasn't even a reason to turn around, that voice alone told me who it was but when I did.

"Here." She said.

"What is this?" I said.

"It's your press pass, and you've to be there right after lunch, therefore I advise you not to drink nothing at all Pope."

"First, I know nothing of this and I'm tired of you and everyone else calling me by my last name, its Mr. Pope or Vice Mayor will do just as fine." 'Do you understand that or do I've to have you to write it 500 times on paper."

I had taking another drink while she stood there looking at me shaking her head like really, if she only knew what I had to deal with this morning. She would've one as well.

"Here, I've other things to do!" 'So take this and the Mayor want you there 15 minutes before the press arrive and change your shirt, you've ring around the collar.

I had taking what she had giving me while looking at her.

"Hey, what is the hell you are wearing, did you just come from the hoe stroll or what and you're going to call me by a proper name, one way or the other Charnel."

I watched her stand there like hooker on the corner with her hands on her hip like if she was advertising p*ssy or something.

"I'll will give you respect when she show it Pope."

"That's enough of your insubordination Charnel, that the last time!" 'You'll give me respect for what I'm!'*

"Really, you've a meeting with the press and that is your second drink, at that what I just witness with my own eyes in less than a few minute."

"This don't count, it's mostly cola and nothing more." I said loudly"

"Sure it is, don't forget your meeting and I put clean shirts in your closet, if I was you." 'I'll use them."

"Anyway, is there anything else Charnel." I ask.

The way she stood there told me that I should've not said nothing just now.

"In fact there is, where you was at last night!"

"Huh."

"Oh, it's like that." 'You playing stupid now?" 'I know you heard every word I just said because the door is closed and there is no one in here but me and you." 'So, where was your black ass last night, I call you nemourios time and not once did you even attempt to call me back or answer your phone."

"Charnel, you can leave now." I said.

I watch her actually leave like a good little secretary would until she gotten an inch from the door, the way she closed it quietly before turning around. I knew she was about to run her mouth.

"What did I do, are you made at me or what?"

I said nothing but pour another drank knowing she wasn't done.

"So, are you mad at me, did I do or say something to hurt you because if I did, then I'm sorry ok."

Charnel just be smart and leave.

"Why is that the answer for everything to you, I waited all night till morning and you couldn't even attempted to call." 'Was you with another woman or something, you know I worry about you, maybe

even more than yourself and I'm always good to you and home when I could be out doing the same thing you are!" 'But I'm at home waiting for you.

"Charnel, listen here." 'I got a very important meeting and I don't have the time for this right now ok."

"Ok, if that how you want to play this game, I'll leave because it's beginning to smell like shit up in here and I know I washed my ass this morning." 'You really can be a bastard and it's amazing how you do it so well."

It was that moment when she turned around, I jumped over my desk and turned her around.

"What she said somewhat loudly."

"Hey you're going to respect me one way or the other Charnel!" I said. "Or what, you're going to fire me!"

The way she stood there without fear or nothing, I turned toward my door and turned on the radio somewhat loudly.

'I'm not going to fire you Charnel, that would be stupid of me but you are going to respect me one way or the other and this is the other."

"What the hell are you going to do to me?"

I don't know where so much anger had come from in the blink of an eye, but I felt the rush when I grabbed her by her arm, it excited me more when she pull away somehow. I grab her again and slam her into my desk, the sound of crap hitting the hardwood floors was louder than loud. That sound alone blinding in with her telling me how I was hurting her, this girl was no borne princess. Charnel fought and earn every penny she had as she fought herself away from me but I wanted more of this.

I grab her once more and over powered her by spinning her around and ripping at her shorter than short skirt. My lung fill with air when I saw the tips of her lightly colored panties, it was like I could hear her breathing while the scent of her moist ass crack and marinated p*ssy fill my nostrils. It could've been nothing more than the way I pull at her shirt, it was like whatever had been building up escape like a crack fish tank before it completely explode from the split between her ass. I wanted to feel my swollen d*ck deep inside her and the more she fought the more I became stronger for her birth p*ssy that I've enjoyed so much but this was different altogether.

15

She tried to yell but I cover her mouth while telling her to shut the f*ck up, I held her tightly while ripping my own pants down, it was like my little man was pushing out on his own. The sight of me forcing her down slowly until my eraction felt like it was going too ripped through her painted. My d*ck was like a mad soldier, it wanted to conquer and ripped the shut up and Charnel p*ssy was it target. The more she squirmed and wiggle the more I wanted the p*ssy to a point that I could get her panties off fast enough.

What was happening to me, why was her p*ssy so heavenly scented but when I entered her body, it wasn't the love making. What I was doing was destroying the p*ssy with every thrust into her hot soft wetness was pouring like ragging river. I don't know who she gotten away but I force her into my desk, it was black p*ssy as far as my eyes could see. I don't know I gotten back inside her that fast but I was, my little man knew what he wanted and not even safe sold protect this p*ssy from the damage I had inflicted until I bust deep in her.

The sound of peoples at the door trying to get in had no effect on me. I held her by her neck white kicking her legs apart, the way I had her pen down by her neck into the oak. I just didn't care about what the f*ck anyone thought. What had just happen, I watched her move slower than ever while gathering her stuff piece by piece until she was somewhat dress.

"Hey, I'm sorry Charnel.

The sight of her saying nothing, she didn't even pushed me away, it was like she was in shock or dis belief as she open the door and there stood my noisy as co-worked looking in like if any of this was their business. I watched the woman cater to her like if this was any of their concern. They had taking her away and all I done before looking at the janitor with keys in his hand.

"Hey you, this is my office!" stay the f*ck out." I told him.

What the f*ck just happen as I grab the entire bottle tuning it upside down like if it was water before sitting down and get back up walking around. So much was on my mind like the way she slapped me before leaving and the way she had accused me of cheating or the way she gotten loud. This was so un-called for when she could've just left like I asked her to, this was some real bullshit and it's not like she haven't giving me the p*ssy before more times than I could count. The thought of me like this unknown adventure really arouse me more than ever, is there more of this out there.

I grab another bottle and turned it up while thinking about Chanel knowing she want do nothing about it. There is no way she was going to lock up this big d*ck to a point that she can't ever have it again. I stop dead in my tracks and the sight of it made me check out myself, there was blood all over me and her bloody pad told me that she was on her period but the more I looked around. She had gotten blood on my floor on my table, and the way it was scattered, she must to gotten it on her hands and every time she tried to pull me out of her must to have left her hand bloody. What a f*cking mess she made up in here, this was some really bullshit tight about now.

Chapter 6

The Speech

I had no ideal about what to say while feeling a little light headed while trying to listen to Charnel but for some strange reason. I couldn't understand a thing she was saying her words seem to be nothing more than jibberish to me. This word glass thingy that was before me looked more blurred than anything to me right now no matter how hard I tried to focus on the tiny little letters that was no looking even more smaller. There was nothing more I could say to myself but what the hail but the sight of the international flags from around the world.

In so many ways it gave me an ideal of what it was and why I was here. I had taking a step back looking around and then toward the audience trying to get myself together before I make a complete ass of myself before these good peoples.

"As we stand here on this great amazing day coming together for a change that will carry us into the next generation of promise because as you." 'I've seen a better tomorrow for me and you and our children's who will someday grow into our future. 'It'll be them who have the ability to grow and become the next generation of true leaders of what represent us today." 'It'll be them who will push us beyond the next great mountain top of our past generations, it will to guide us because of their stability that will drive us to a better future of tomorrow because it was a dream that had been giving to me by the Almighty."

It was that moment I felt Charnel bumping me more than normal as it made me wonder what the hail she wanted now. The sight of her sitting there made her look so sexy to a point that I could see her camel toe and visualized my face between her fat hairy p*ssy lips that was bigger than my own lips. It was the perfect match and I so needed a drink right now while I glanced over at Jordon wo o made contact with after listening to him tell his little white hoe how much of an idiot that I was. He didn't even care that I had hear him from the way he looked at me with such arrogance. This white boy really was a little uppity blue eyed bastard, he need a few straps across his back or a good ass f*cking to bring him down off his high horse.

It was that moment I felt myself getting hotter while whipping my face that seem like nothing more than alcohol expiring from me. I had taking several deep breaths that echoed throughout the area from the microphone picking up every last sound including the loud machine gun type farts that escape my ass no matter how hard I held my butt cheeks together. Charnel had continue pulling on me while one of the nemourios Priest stood up trying to steal my spotlight but I told myself that it wasn't going to happen.

We both stood before everyone going back and forth as I wipe my face with my sleeve several times. This wasn't no catholic event or at least it didn't look like one. He had eventually gotten the message and just stood there smiling at the crown like if this was his church or something.

"Peoples as I stand before you being rudely interrupt by the Father here who can bless all you later but we must move forward within our growth." 'It alone can't be done just by us along but it is because of men's like these who stand before me and you and us." Fore it's them who're the representatives of God, the almighty who lives within all of us because it's our faith as I look at all these flags of many nations hanging high and above of these great brick wall of this great structure." 'It's you who stand before representing your country of this world, it's you who stand before me in your black suits."

'Your presence alone is the reason why we can all come together as one making this bright sunny day a peace of the world history...our history of loyalty and faith and prosperity." 'I stand before all of you giving you my word of good will and good health and living in this land of plenty of growth and equality while glancing at the glass thingy while focusing on the word mental saying to myself...what the hell."

I had continue to talking while Charnel was now really tugging at me none stop until she had gotten up pushing me aside like if I was nothing but a child or something. The alcohol I drank before had me staggering a little, until felt someone pushing on me a little more taking over the microphone while Charnel pull me completely to the rear. She had totally disrespected me for the position I held looking at that little smart ass kid been introduce by one of his little boy f*ck buddies.

"Hi everyone…my name is Mr. Daniel L. Jordon and me and my team are representative of America who made this possible on this great day of togetherness." 'America is grateful to be a part of this unity of one."

It was that moment I stood up while Charnel tried to pull me back down because I has something else I needed to say but I ended up falling into him almost knocking him down but he caught himself. I ended up falling but Charnel had come to aid and gotten me away from that area. We ended up in the car unknowing how I had gotten home or even undress for that matter.

Chapter 7

Mayor Insanity

That following morning I had awaken looking at the news wondering what the hell was going on after taking several deep breaths knowing this was far from being over. The moment I had arrived to the office becoming the center of everyone attention only old me that I starred up the hornets' nest. The only thing that came to mind was the word vengeance for some strange reason.

"Good morning Charnel." I said.

The look in her eye wasn't good from the way her eyes never left the sight of me.

"The boss want to see you ASAP like now." Charnel said in a low tone of voice.

"Why?" I ask.

"Maybe your big day view yesterday and you're late. Charnel said never taking her eyes from me.

It was almost lunch time from the antique brass clock that stood in the center of the room up high for everyone to see. I had almost panic when I felt someone tapping me on the shoulder without warning of any kind.

"Oh, it's you Ms. Glasco...What?" I said loudly.

"Mayor would like to see you like now." She said looking all big breasted and thick as hell in all the right places knowing as much as I didn't want to see her this morning.

The sight of her body always told me that she got some warm good stuff down there.

"Ok!" I replied while informing her to let him know that I'm on my way.

"Well, Mr. It good that you decided to come in when you want." Pointing her long witch like finger at the clock.

It was nothing more than a cheap shot at me but I said nothing back because she know nothing of my business. She stood there watching me walk to my office knowing that I was the vice mayor and I should've put her in her place before leaving. This was just too much for me to handle and way too early for her crap knowing I needed a good strong drink right about now. My bar was such a beautiful sight of some of the world finest liquor county money can buy.

The first drop hit my mouth was like paradise as those Germans sure does know something about good whisky. It was nothing but perfection as I poured another before sitting down while still savoring the way it went down so smooth and satisfying. My ass felt so good in my fat man leather chair as I had to sip my drink and prepare myself for a hard day's work. The thought of what the Mayor wanted looking at the many scatted folders on my desk was nothing more than mind bothering causing me to sit deeper.

"Hey wake up!" It was Charnel.

"The Mayor wants to see you now...pronto!" 'Get your drunk ass up now!" She yell like if she didn't have no dam sense at all.

The door was left wide open as I gotten up looking at everyone looking in on me before I closed it myself while informing her that she is not going to keep talking to me like im nobody. It was that moment that I gotten myself together about to take a quick shoot listening to Charnel say

"Really...you can't be serious."

The moment I walked in I saw Mr. High Mighty sitting there but when I attempted to sit.

"Who told you sit down?" Mayor Phillips

I had done nothing but gotten back up looking at him shaking his head back and forth twiddling his thumbs like if he had no patients for me at all.

"So, what do you've to say for yourself?"

"Mayor, sir?" I responded.

"Don't play stupid with me this morning because my phone has been ringing none stop and that not counting at my own house!"

"Mayor, what're you talking about?"

It was that moment I watch him pick up the remote as we watch the morning tapped news, I knew what he was talking about from the beginning.

"Mayor, I was feeling good that day or something." I said.

"You wasn't feeling good because you were drunk off your ass on national TV." 'It was a simple assignment and all you had to do was read from the teleprompter and nothing more but you made a fool of me and yourself... in front of the media" Mayor Phillips responded loudly.

I stood there looking down at him while wanting to sit down, this wasn't a good day but I knew that when I first walked into this place.

"You know, I have had enough of you and your intelligence level or at least you should've some."

There was nothing I could really say looking at the screen he kept playing repeatedly like if I wanted to see it again. The sight of Ms. Glasco was enjoying every moment of this with her big tities busting from her chest while smirking. The sight of him yelling at me when I turned away from it looking around the room, it was so uncalled for. This man was treating me like some kind of kid or something that I was not, im a grown ass man known if he continue to act immature. I was leaving this unprofessional behavior.

"So what do you think about this." The Mayor ask.

"Mayor, I wasn't feeling good that day sir."

"Why wasn't you feeling well Mr. Pope?"

"I was a little dizzy, even before I left sir."

"Are you dizzy now?" The, Mayor ask.

I watched him shove several awaiting papers in my hand the minute he stood up aggressively.

"What is this Mayor?" I ask.

"Read it." He shouted loudly just before sitting back down with his veins popping out of his head.

I watched him sit back down while I looked over the papers he had just giving me while taking a seat.

"Who ask you to sit down?" The, Mayor ask.

I just looked at him.

"Really Mayor?" I stated.

"Get up and out of my chair until I tell you that you can sit." The, Mayor said aggressively.

I had done what he said this man had some real issues.

"I want you to pay special attention at Mr. Jordon commit of your behavior."

I wasn't even amazed knowing I should've been but for some strange reason I wasn't.

"Were you aware that you were supposed to cut the ribbon and those Priest wasn't all catholic, they were from around the world." He said calmly.

The sight of him look like he had gotten himself all work up looking tired, this man needed something to lift him up, maybe Ms. Glasco was going to bend that big ass over for him when I'm the hell up out of here.

"What am I going to do with you?" Mayor ask.

There wasn't much I could say while standing, my feet's was beginning to hurt listening to him repeat himself like if he really wanted an answer back but he did.

"Mayor, what am I to do sir...what done is done."

"Why're you even here anymore...you're not the same man I had by myside tears ago." 'What happen to you is all I'm asking."

I said nothing in response.

"Listening here, there was so many peoples there...you had a simple task to perform and look what you done...you sat us back to slavery with your ignorant and everyone in the world watched how ignorant you made us look. 'You're in the spotlight now and you've to be aware because you represent what we're.

"Mayor, my apologies for what I done but like I said, it wasn't a good day for me."

He sat there looking knowing there was nothing else for me to say regarding what has already happen and from the look in his face. This man wanted me out of his office from his expression knowing I didn't want to be here anyway. I watched him get up walking toward me after he told me to sit down, he moved toward with a slow stroll like if he was thinking the entire time. His hand trailed his expensive oak desk, it was a gift to him from some foreign investor who had it hand delivered from Sweden.

He stopped looking at me like if I was about to be punished like some little boy by his dad or something but even I knew that wasn't going to happen. I felt him pushing down on my shoulder causing me to move around, my mind had gone into the world of deep thought.

"Mr. Pope, I want you to take some time off." He said. he had giving me this strange odd feeling when I felt him breathing down my neck heavily while asking me if I had been drinking."

"No, Mayor, it's too early for that sir." I said in a whisper tone to of voice.

I wondered how he could tell when Charnel made sure I rinse my mouth and sprayed cologne she pulled from my desk. She told me what she thought he wanted with me, the sight of Ms. Busy Noisy Body gotten my attention while holding her notebook like if she was doing something important. At least she could have giving me flash or peep show since she knew I was looking trying to get at least a glimpse of that hairy bush she was concealing. She didn't allow that thang to get a pinch of air from the way her legs was close air tight.

This woman always gave off the image that her life was just perfect, maybe it was since she stayed so professional and private with that little short stubby husband. He wasn't pounding that thang the way I would, she was too much woman for a little man. This woman needed the buck, she wasn't no different from any other that bleeds like the rest of her species. Her shit smell just like mines as she glanced at the Mayor like if I was nothing more than a problem, shit for all I know.

She probably just giving his married ass the panties minutes ago behind closed doors that are never open during their meeting. She only needed a real n*gga deep in her like me, there want be no babysitting in my game. Her destiny would be getting the long and strong…the child support maker…the divorce separator…the 12 inch killer is what she could be experiencing the love producer.

"Hey are you listening to me?" Mayor ask

"Sir." I responded back.

"I want you to take some time off like now!" Mayor said politely.

"Mayor." I responded back.

"Now, Mr. I want you off these grounds today."

I so wanted to tell him to go f*ck himself but because I wasn't his child to be yelling at but what would that have done. He was already highly upset.

"Mayor, it not my vacation time yet." I said mildly.

"Yes it is he shouted…starting now like right this minute.

"Mayor, I don't have the time to take leave because I used them and all my sick time."

I could see Ms. Know It All playing with her little computer toy while voicing her opinion that I had a few leaves days on the record. There wasn't much to say after listening to her but.

"Mayor, those few days that I do have is being saved for a rainy day sir."

It was that moment he looked at me, his strong old fat hands pushed on my shoulder even harder knowing I sank several inch into the chair.

"Mr. Pope, we're longtime friends right?" Mayor ask.

I knew he was looking at Ms. Know It All long legs from the direction of his voice.

"We're like family right, your dad was one of my best good friends and the same as you were a kid, I looked out for you and now I'm doing it now." 'Don't worry about the vacation or sick time my friend, I want you to take some time off and get your head right and when you return, it will be like old times sake."

"What about Charnel?" I ask since no one was fund of her up in here.

He told me how she could be assign to Ms. Glasco and how she will be alright until I return from my time off.

"I'll take care of all the paperwork, you want even have to sigh out, just leave now…like within the hour."

"How long Mayor?"

I watch him move about knelling down by his b*tch of a secretary barley touching her knew…it along told me that they had something on the down low by the way she didn't even flinch an inch and he is supposed to be so dam righteous family man and all…niggas be doing the foulest shit. And he got to be al up in her face with my business, shit I'm the vice mayor…shit if I drop a few slugs in his old wrinkle ass. I become the mayor overnight and I don't give a shit about him knowing me when I was a youngin as he calls me.

"Mr.' how does two weeks sound?" Mayor ask.

It wasn't like I had a choice noticing her looking at his ass walking toward me…probably even creaming in her panties right now and it wasn't over me.

"Sure, Mayor…sound great sir." I said.

"You know what, let make it three and when you return…you'll be a new man." Mayor Phillips said.

This man acted as if he just won the lottery or something, there wasn't much for me to do at this point but get up and walk away. I had been stopped before I gotten out.

"We've to make this official, even more with the media wanting to know every inch of business that happen in here." Mayor stated.

I listen to him order his secretary to call in Charnel, it had only taking a second before she arrived she should've been college educated. Charnel had a way of sensing what was going on from the initials start, she was just smart like that. It only took her one glance to see what was going on as I could here a few more being called in as well. We watched Mr. Watson, the 3rd in Command stand before the mayor as he raised his hand to take his temporary Oath of Allegiance.

The sight of Charnel looking on should've been shocking but in reality, the life she had been living. I personally don't think anything was surprising to her anymore, it was like if she saw this coming before I did knowing she had no psychic abilities or should could be working for one of my hot line call center. Well not a real one, just mostly single mothers with a phone line in their apartment. It was nothing more than extra money knowing who ever call would never call again but at least we got them once.

It was all a profit, the sight of everyone now shaking hand told me that it was over that fast.

"Welcome aboard Vice Mayor Watson."

This was nothing more than some bullshit as I never recall him giving me respect of any kind, it was me that put his fast old ass in the big seat. This n*gga does need to feel the pop-pop with the quickness but darkness always surface to light when you least expect it. The sight of Charnel now shaking hands with the rest of these hypocrites.

"I want a meeting with you ASAP." Ms. Glasco said to Charnel.

It was that moment I watch everyone leave there way, it was that moment that I just gotten relieve of my job like if I was nothing more than a stripper hoe. My blood pressure had rising to almost explosion.

"Is that what I'm to you, even now?"

Charnel had said after over hearing me speaking to myself as I said nothing in return but looked at her leaving toward my office. I had made myself a drink before sitting down, it was what I needed right now feeling violated looking at her walk through the door looking upset. The sight of her standing before made me want to take her like right now, this very second.

"What is wrong with you?" Charnel ask somewhat loudly.

"Nothing, is there anything I can do for you Charnel?" I ask.

The sight of her running off at the mouth talking about respect that I should be giving her for many reason while moving closer as if I couldn't hear her at all.

"Hey what the hell did you do that for you bastard!" She yell louder than she should have.

It was me that took her from that stage and made her a lady of dignity and if I wanted the p*ssy, it was mine whenever I wanted it.

"Are you happy now, does that make you feel better, you didn't have to rip my panties like that!"

The sight of her holding them had giving me no remorse for what I just done and it wouldn't have happen if she would've just let me gently removed them from the beginning.

*"This is all your fault Charnel and why was you smiling in Watson face?" 'You want to f*ck him for the next couples of weeks while I'm going, are you going to be dancing for him behind closed doors now that I'm going and I notice how you made your way toward him all happy and shit."*

"You really are stupid aren't you and you drink to dame much and even more at work, why is that?"

"What do you care about what I do and you haven't answer my question about Watson?" Not realizing that I had gotten that loud when I told her to lower hers only seconds ago.

"That why you're losing your job!" Charnel yell.

This words sent chill down my spine, this stripper knows more than what I thought.

"Hey!" 'Wait, you knew of this?" She said nothing back, even when I yell at her several times more.

I took several more quick drinks straight from the bottle, my inside burned from the 90 proof and just like that she went into the door before hitting the floor harder than what I intended. She must to have gotten up coming at me like some wild cat knowing this wasn't the place for this bullshit but she didn't care. Charnel was crazy like that, she was ghetto born while she fill my mouth with blood from her ignorance until we heard knocking on the door. It was that moment that she stop her none sense while I limp toward the door must to have been a sight for the mayor to see asking us if everything was alright. His staff looked on as well.

"Charnel, are you ok?" The she b*tch ask.

The sight of all of us now looking at Charnel black silky panties on the floor as we watched her make her way toward them like a mother to a child. The mayor look intensely without blinking once. This man had no idea what was going on between us nor did anyone else, they looked at me like if I was the guilty n*gga or something. It had only taking security a moment to arrive looking at me crazily.

It was like if no one had respect for me or even concern for my wellbeing noticing several of them now standing round like if they wanted to arrest a n*gga or something. Since they were white, they must to have been taught that at KKK University while Charnel said nothing no matter how many question Ms. Glasco kept asking her. The sight of my badly injured leg wasn't even brought up from the way she was using my leg like a soccer ball as I was barely able to stand.

"Meet me in my office now." Mayor instructed me.

It was very unprofessional of him yelling at me the way he just done before walking away like if he was participating in some walk-a-thon like if he was coming up from the rear or something. Once inside he had walk out only returning slamming his squeaky door behind him the hurted my ears knowing that security wasn't far behind him right now or waited outside just in case I had to get up in his old wrinkle ass. I was already seated looking at him instruct me to get my black ass up while he stood over me looking pregnant with his massive over weight stomach hanging over his belt like Santa.

"Mayor you need to relax before you've a heart attack up in here sir and what you saw isn't what you think before you even start making accusation that you might regret sir."

"Really!" 'Then maybe you can explain what I just saw as well as the rest of the staff members."

"Mayor' you heard her tell you secretary that nothing happen and from that…what else can I say on my behalf."

"Listen you little snake in the grass, you seem to have an answer for everything every sense you were a little boy and you are doing the same thing as a man!" 'When're you going to grow up and accept responsibility for what you do?"

I stood there looking down on this man saying nothing to him.

"Ok, remain silence but one day you're going to pay for all the wrong you do daily and you must think that you're so brilliant that none of us just saw how you rape your own secretary or baby moma or whatever you call her!" 'You'll pay someday and it's sad to say but I hope I'm there to see you fall…enough is enough don't you think?"

I said nothing back as he sat there twiddling his thumbs looking at me without a smile in sight asking me if I think that all of them are just stupid altogether or just dummies. There was nothing to say to this man from this point on, shit I'm not even supposed to be here right now that I think about it.

"No, Mayor, we're all very smart sir." I responded looking down on him adjusting his hemorrhoids ass.

I watched him get up while digging in his ass talking about what just happen saying that he hope it don't become a public embarrassment if this should happen to get passed these door. He told me how my days are numbered in this profession and how he always known that I don't have what it takes to be a leader and how I was always nothing more than a taker ever since I was a little kid. He yell louder about how that what I was while interrupting me every time I had a chance to talk in my defense. I just wanted to leave while he must to have call Security inside standing like little good house niggas while he walked outside like if I needed babysitting or something.

Shit, im a grown ass man with authority, I stood looking at both of them who said nothing regardless of what I said to them, even my jokes wasn't even funny to them.

"Can you please be quiet sir" One of them said.

I needed a drink after hearing that while laughing at these uneducated minimum wage rent a cops, as started looking around for his stash coming up with nothing.

"Sir could you remain still please." One of them said.

I had done nothing but started laughing even more like wow knowing they knew who I was the entire time, they were funny, even more when one of them mention how they may have to take me down. I remain doing what I wanted until the sound of the Mayor yelling.

"What the hell is going on in here?"

But when he realized what was happen, he said nothing in my defense.

"Get him out of here." Mayor yell.

I had been escorted out but the sight of Charnel now standing near several flash light wanna be cops, she didn't even look my way or even speak this time. I kept calling her name while been force out the door until I was out.

"Go home and cool off or the next time it will be the police department that you'll be dealing with you." Guard said.

As I stood looking at them. Hearing the sound of police cars pulling up as I had been asked to standby but when it was all said and done. They had told me to go home as well noticing the mayor and his new assistance looking on, it would've been nice to see charnel before leaving but maybe it was best that we didn't. I probably would of hoe checked her in front of everyone and that may resulted me in handcuff. She had scratched me up like a cat and no one said nothing of it as someone had giving me my key and coat.

Chapter 8

Home Sweet Home

I had arrived home and it been several days of drinking throughout thinking that I should be relaxing but I was doing the opposite. The decision of another had gave me this time to think while hoods mostly found their way toward my door. What was done in the street was now face to face one after another while I somewhat missed the political life but it was only temporarily. I so wanted to visit but the mayor himself told me that he would personally see to it that I'm arrested on the spot for trespassing.

Even though he laugh, his big bottom ass would do it just because he can as I taking another look at the fountain of youth walking from the bathroom drying her hands in a skirt so small that her butt cheeks was displayed very well bouncing about.

"Hey, can I make you something to eat like a sandwich or something. Stacy said.

"You can make me some real food like a full course dinner." I said loudly.

She just stood there looking at me like if she didn't understand what I just said but how much do I expect for a girl who could be my daughter.

"I'm good ok…thanks anyway but you can make me another rum and cola." I responded.

"Ok…daddy is that all you want?" Stacy said.

I just looked at her walk away knowing that was all I wanted for now, this girls was taking every bit of sperm from my body but I made sure that her virgina wasn't going to process a drop of it as I made sure if it didn't go down her throat, it was rubbed into her ass or stomach by my own hands.

"What did you say daddy." Stacy responded.

I said nothing, she overheard me talking to myself as I wondered if she knew what home meant, she wasn't supposed to be here this long. This was basically a simple booty for dope transaction and it been nearly 4 days that she has been here, eating sleeping drinking and running up my toilet bill with her hourly bladder. The sight of her eating while she grabbed a pillow placing it in front of her saying how she didn't want to display her full stomach while saying how embarrassment it was.

"Hey, don't look at my stomach. Stacy said.

"How can I see your stomach with all those cloths you are wearing?"

It was that moment…she stood up looking down at me after taking another bite.

"You think I'm wearing too many cloths daddy?" Stacy ask.

I said nothing as I watched her take a drink of beer, she instantly started removing her cloths until she was in her panties and bra and still asking me if she was wearing too much.

"You look fine, there was nothing more to say as she continue to eat." I said.

"I'll just hold in my stomach if I start to look fat ok daddy." Stacy responded.

This young woman had some serious daddies issues within her, she probably never had one so she clings to man willing to show her attention. I really didn't care, it works out for me for right now I guess, while watching her flip thru channels.

"So is everything taking care of?" I ask.

She said nothing back while covering her stomach up with the pillow after she was doing eating as I ask her again but it seem like if she had gotten upset or something.

"Yea!" Stacy responded once more.

The sight of her laughing made me wonder about what was so funny.

"Stacy, im trying to get you paid, the county is never going to take this to court, it a fast settlement and remember that white girl will be paid more" 'You need to be strong and do everything as planed!" I shouted.

"Ok! 'Don't yell at me anymore." Stacy shouted back.

I watch her drop the pillow while doing her hair in two girlie like pony tails.

"Remember this is several month planning and we just gotten our new budget and elections are not far away for that clown of a mayor who wants to be re-elected...meaning he will settle this overnight and if all fails you are going to say how I hurt you emotionally, ok." I explained.

"Yea, I do just relax and Karen knows the entire plain. Stacy said.

"So when ae we going to celebrate?" Stacy ask. "Celebrate what?" I ask.

"This plan to make it official, we can do it shortly when Karen gets here." Stacy said.

I gotten up when the doorbell rang.

"Oh, that might be my girl, celebration time!" Stacy said loudly.

I watched her answer it as they both kiss before she let her in.

"What kind of freaky shit is this, it was all I could say to myself."

She was amazing with each step she made into my home, they had both taking sat side by side for a moment.

"Nice house, you must got some big dollas for such luxury, can I've a tour please." Karen ask.

"You joking right Karen, how many time have you been through this place?" I ask.

"But since you're in the laughing mode, are you sure you know what to do and are you feeling strong about doing this?" I ask.

"Ok, im joking but you need to relax...you are always so serious." Karen said.

"Stacy check your girl, this is like a 500.000 payday between the two of you and she had jokes!" I said.

"What the hell, let do the tour." I yelled.

It's only a tour but the sight of my bedroom made them always giggle, it wasn't long after we all gotten comfortable with each other.

"Hey, im taking my girl to your bedroom?" Stacy said.

"May I ask why?" I said.

"You may not but you can up in a few minutes and see why im asking." Stacy replied.

They both started kissing none stop.

"Enough of this." Stacy said.

"Did I do something wrong?" Karen ask.

"Are you still my b*tch." Stacy ask.

"Yes…always." Karen replied.

"Then let's go upstairs." Stacy said.

I watch her grab her by her hand pulling her with her.

"Hey don't you for get to b ring the d*ck for our celebration." Stacy said smiling.

I made myself another drink feeling a little nervous about this plan while sitting back knowing I was already drunk enough before fallen asleep.

"Hey wakeup you missing all the fun." Stacy said.

That moment I felt her lightly touching my hand while looking upstairs.

"Let's go baby." Stacy said.

I felt her pulling at me until I gotten up watching her backside jiggle from her slow movement up the stairs twitching that ass.

"Mum girl that look so yummy." I said.

The thought of missing all of this yumminess going on under my roof, I was nothing more than a dam fool looking at her friend in her panties.

"You two are real eyes openers if I must truly so." I responded.

Stacy walk toward her friend locking lips until she waved for me to come closer.

"Karen, this is my friend and now yours hopefully." Stacy said.

"I'm both of your friends…in fact best friend." I responded

Karen passed Stacy the joint she just lithe and she gave it to me after several puffs and Stacy took it from my hand. We passed it around until it was going while they were having a breast grabbing contest while locking lips.

"You young ladies are giving me a sight to remember." I said while laughing.

Stacy pulled me in closer to their circle of passion, it was still so early in the morning and I haven't even wash my nuts from last night and now I was about to be between both of them from how this was going. Stacy pulling me in closer while Karen just look until she push both of us together into this long passionate none stop kiss. Her lips was like a sister but softer as well as her tender touching was amazing to me as if she was enjoying every second. Stacy join in as we were all in this weird type of kissing all at once but it was very different feeling them caressing my back the entire time.

The way Stacy had taking my hand placing it on Karen soft breast while she done the same with Karen hand on my crotch. Her touch sent chills throughout my body and I enjoyed every second of it, it was almost indescribable. I swear the best loves is always the first from the moans, the sound of Stacy voice was actual making her friend more comfortable even though it didn't seem to be needed. Karen was a slut in the making from her experience touches.

I've done so much in the sexual world but never with someone I known since she was probably in diapers, even though she was legal. Her dad had every right to rip my head completely off but I guess right now it doesn't matter. I just have to deal with that when the situation presents itself I reckon because I was about to be in her zone. Her darken red hair was so attractive to me along with her perfectly red lips that I couldn't stop kissing.

Nothing but softness at its best with her darken brown eyes, my imagination of me looking into them while pounding her bareback nonstop. So much young freshness feeling Stacy pulling us apart the moment she separated herself looking at both of us.

"Relax…you look like you trying to devour her." Stacy shouted.

Too much excitement as I needed her to know that my door was open, even if she didn't come with Stacy as I lithe another joint. They were both on cloud nine from how they started laughing when they saw me looking down telling my little man to relax.

"He is fine, you need to relax, don't you know you've two too take care of before it is all said and done." Stacy said.

Both girls just looked at me funny but only if they knew what my crotch area was saying to me.

"Are you talking to your d*ck." Karen ask.

She just heard Stacy say I hope he likes vagina because there enough of it here as we all laughed knowing time would give the answer. She reached into her hand bag pulling out another joint as we smoke it until nothing existed. Stacy and Karen begin undressing each other until Stacy laid back pulling Karen on top of her, both of them had given me a new sense of excitement like never before. Such a sight to see as they entangle like snakes becoming one.

Stacy eyes were upon me as she waved me into their circle of lust kissing party of warm bodies looking at two booties. They wrestled with each other but there was something about Stacy on her back with her hips spreaded almost overtaking my king size bed. Karen soft jiggling humps had sight of her own, she was more slender in a curvy way. Stacy was all sista, her body alone was the reason why I was attracted and women like her is the reason why men can't have just one maybe it was me overall.

But sh*t im not married and with the sights of her coming my way all the time, why should I be, both of these young adult ladies hasn't even truly blossom yet. They will be giving it away for years to come before that happen. But tonight im getting mines knowing both of these flowers are mines watching Karen raise up as if I had scared her while Stacy looked my way.

"Are you okay?"

How could I tell them that I saw two hands coming from my crotch area unzipping my pants listening to my little man telling me that. If I wasn't going to let him out, then he was going to do it himself but that moment I could do nothing but rejoin them looking at what was unbelievable right in front of me. They were both taking their time undressing each other, it was a sight to see. I didn't even get the opportunity to see Karen front panty print, it tells all about a woman from the way Stacy had pull them to her knees. Her body was like looking at a perfect shaped hourglass, thick in the ass and narrow in the waste line.

Stacy started kissing Karen while going south had to have been nothing more than delicious trail to follow, but as I tried.

"Stop!" Stacy said.

I was allowed to kiss up top but my eyes couldn't stop glancing south, Karen looked so delicious while my hand had even been stop by Stacy.

"Touch yourself for right now." Stacy yelled.

It was some freaky turn on that she wasn't going to get from me while there moaning were nothing more than beautiful music to my ears that I wanted to be a part of. I moved in again.

"You can do nothing but watch." Stacy yelled while laughing.

My little man kept telling me to take the p*ssy and that I was the man and how can I let vagina boss me around.

"You feel so good." Karen said to Stacy.

She had to be so right from the way Stacy body just wiggle like if heaven was about her from her many sexual sounds while she buried herself between Karen's yumminess.

"Stacy you devour me so well." Karen said while moaning.

It made me feel like I was nothing and I so wanted to prove that she was in a man's zone and that I was the titleholder in that never ending ring. The way she was enjoying herself only told me that she wasn't given me the opportunity at her belt. It was just wrong altogether smelling nothing but Stacy in the air, maybe it was Karen to but she hasn't been penetrated yet. Not even a finger, the sight of Stacy looking back.

She allowed me to get closer but it wasn't good enough for my little man.

"You are a punk and act like I got a pair and take control of this situation." My little man yelled.

He had become like an iron pole wanting to be in something like now.

"You are torturing me, at least give me a chance to see what happening." Little man ask.

That moment Stacy undone my pants allowing Karen to take him fully into her mouth, amazing sight while pushing me from the back to get closer. Stacy didn't want me inside her yet.

"You got some serious issues young lady." I said.

But I had no choice but to go alone with whatever she wanted.

"Thank you." My little man said.

Every time Karen gave him air rubbing her face with him while Stacy buried herself deeply in Karen, it was wishful thinking of what she was doing knowing I had the find a way to get control of myself. Karen was going to end, perfection at its best.

"Karen you hold the championship belt."

Stacy couldn't even compete, Karen was nothing more than a mystery that I wanted to experience repeatedly. Stacy looked at me knowing she hasn't made me feel like while reaching for Karen's arms as I wondering what the hell she was doing. In the blink of an eye, she was on her back while Karen was now deep in her jungle, it only took a second before Stacy pulled my face into her. This was so unreal, something I thought that would never happen any time soon, my little man was now like a cannon ready to explode on Karen's.

We seem to be both driving Stacy crazy from her wild movement, she almost thrown us from the bed a long with herself. Stacy screamed to the top of her voice causing my little man nearly pushed me up off the bed.

"You are an ass hogging bastard." My little man said.

I ignore him while Karen tightly wrapped hands around him, it wasn't enough…this little uncontrollable fool wanted more or he was going to do something stupid. That moment I moved up toward Karen, Stacy caught notice pushing me back to her jungle. Maybe if I just let him get near the couchie.

"Either you stay down there until I tell you that you are done or you can stand away from us and watch until I tell you that you can joined back in." Stacy said aggressively.

Participation was better than nothing is all I could come up with as I went back to work doing what I could, the sight of Karen ass looking at me made me wanted to penetrate. I found myself slipping a finger or two inside playing with her juiciest and sniff-sniff from time to time, my little man wanted more but he was satisfied for the moment it seem. It was some real bullshit but something was better than nothing at all. Karen had went back to her hand job as I so wanted to tell her to just stop but I couldn't.

It was better to just let it happen as her hands was so soft and warm, amazing is all I could think while I place my hand under Stacy big booty knowing I was about to explode. It was that moment I felt Karen doing something different, she had buried her tongue between the cracks of Stacy ass like if she was aiming for her poop-shooter. She had left me all alone before coming up for air lip locking with me, the thought of what she had done wasn't to my approval but I couldn't resist the fragrance she had acquired. The sight Stacy now bouncing off the floor displaying her big humps was like steak to hungry man.

Karen had caught me looking while smiling afterwards, it was that moment she forced me into Stacy big chocolate ass. It was like some sort of turn on.

"Eat all that booty n*gga!" Karen yell.

I should have been offended from the way she said it but she was nothing more than a young adult too know what real raci'sm was all about.

This was nothing but playfulness at it kinkiest and somewhat turn on to me and I tore into her like a race car winning the 500. That moment I felt her slide beneath me causing me to explode in her mouth, this nasty little b*tch consumed it like if she was starving for it. I could only hope that this wasn't done watching her approach Stacy, she locked lips, it was nasty as we were all in my birthday suits.

"Yumminess." Stacy said loudly.

I assume it was over, my little man was somewhat satisfied and the girls seem to got what they wanted but it wasn't.

"Are you my b*tch!" Stacy ask Karen.

I saw what I couldn't even imagine as I watch Stacy swish my sperm throughout her mouth while looking at Karen. They now stood face to face.

"Oh shit." Is all I could say.

I saw what I could even imagine as she grabbed Karen by the back of her hair pulling her backwards while releasing my semen into her mouth.

"Swallow it you little nasty one." I said while laughing.

These two young ladies was nothing more than freaks at their best. I don't know why one minute we were all laughing and goofing off but my back was turned toward the door. Karen had this look in her eyes like if she saw a ghost or something becoming as quiet as a mouse. I had no idea what was going on with her but she has screened her loudest.

Stacy said nothing as she looked at me like if someone was standing behind me but I knew that couldn't be. My doors was locked but that very moment it sounded like Charnel voice shouting at me. It cause me to turn around but before I could, I had been blindsided by something heavy forcing me to the floor. It was like I had instantly went into another world of pain seen stars before my face.

My sight had been blur feeling something hit me again taken me back to the floor, it was like as if I was completely out. I tried to get up while struggling to feel what was a round me, the sight of Charnel long legs as I tried to talk. My words had been slurred badly somehow to a point that I couldn't even understand myself or even hear good right now.

"You nasty little b*tches…you both have less than a second to get your shit and get the f*ck out of my house!" Charnel yelled.

I felt her kick me once more with her pointed boots, it felt like she busted my ribs or something feeling the bed move aggressively by the sound of the springs as I did my best to get away from her voice.

"Stop, stop, stop!" I kept yelling.

I somehow felt my way toward the wall but I had been hit by something else before it hit the wall breaking on contact. This was for sure Charnel from the way she acted the last time we gotten into it over a woman that was nothing more than a friend. I felt her kick me several more times as I grabbed her legs trying to get her to stop but somehow she gotten loose.

"Charnel stop!" I kept yelling.

The sound of the girls running down the wooden stairs would have been like drums to me if my hearing wasn't damaged. They apologize entire time until they could be heard anymore, they left me like I was nothing but even I knew they couldn't take on Charnel. She was just ghetto born from multiple generations as I seen her fight many girls at one time and never back down from anyone.

"You dirty cheating lying bastard, you rape me in your office only days ago and now you're f*cking these b*tches in our home… our bed!"

Charnel kept kicking me, I was in so much pain while hearing another voice telling her to stop before she do something that she regrets.

"I could've press charges on you and even the mayor had told me about the publicity that was to follow if I did." Charnel shouted.

She had told me how everyone was looking out for me and I was too stupid to realize when people was trying to protect me from all the dirt I was doing.

"You're nothing no more than a lowlife and all your dirt is going to catch up to you someday bastard." She yelled while kicking me again.

I could feel myself bleeding of warm blood covered my body while coughing up blood as well while gasping for air. My sight was nearly gone a long with my hearing as I felt like passing out any second now.

"Charnel, let's go, this n*gga ain't shit and he never will be!"

It was Tasha ghetto black ass.

"You know stray dogs don't belong to know one and that what his trifling ass is…a stray dog humping anything in sight girl!" Tasha said loudly.

She talk shit the entire time, even while she knelled down by me.

"I'm done with your lying cheating black ass while throwing my house key at me." Charnel yelled.

I watched her walk away before I pass out.

Chapter 9

Clinic

I had awaken days later the sight of the medical equipment could be seen as plain as more sun shining through my window. The awful taste in my mouth was as if I've been eating a bowl shit or something, it was horrible even my bad breath had to have been the worse ever. My lips felt chap, the sight of a *Medical Staff Member* walking near passing me by saying.

"Hey maun awh yoa awake me sei."

I had no idea what this dread head just said to me, this place has some of the worst medical care and looking at him see why.

"You come over here."

I had gotten his attention watching him come closer to me.

"Ya maun… what mei do foe yua maun Mr. Poupe." He said while putting my chart back in his space after looking at my name or something.

The thought of him doing that told me that he didn't even take the time to learn my name, what kind the staff member was he knowing those nasty looking alone hanging dreadlocks can't be regulation and if it is. This hospital needs to be more professional and I had to tell him watching him stand there looking oddly like you never been told how unprofessional he look. I shook my head back and forth looking at him standing in front of me saying.

"Mei vary busi maun…whut yoa wanna maun!" this dread-head said.

"This can't be your professional luck." I said.

"What you maun... ya sick...yoa neadz toa getz betta aund pai yoa bill and getz out plus maun...thiz isz mei family medical estazbelisment, its likz Americaun Presizdent Obame medicaul care and yoa havz toa manuy visators toa muach. Wez shoauld makz theum pai to visuit youa maun." He said.

I watched him check my blood pressure and other things while talking nonstop the entire time before leaving saying.

"Yoa noa nouthing abouat nouthing maun." He said.

The way he kept looking back made me wonder about how in the hell did I end up in this dump of a place knowing from the way he was so aggressive. That this dread head didn't give a shit about me while listening to him talk about nothing plus I can understand a word coming from his mouth.

"Good morning." It was Charnel, she had walked in immediately after that dread had left.

He had turned his head to catch a glimpse of her backside smiling afterwards. It was that moment he looked at me and shook his head while mumbling something that I couldn't hear. I was speechless looking at her standing there like if nothing had happened between us only days ago wondering what the hell she wanted.

"What do you want rib breaker?" I said.

"Be nice to you baby momma." She said softly while asking me how I was feeling this Godly morning.

"I feel like shit and is all because of you." I said.

I watched her pace back and for in front of me while holding her nose from my constant gas passing.

"I brought you some things." Watching her pull hygiene stuff from her bag.

It was my stuff from my house and some close that she had placed on an awaiting hanger, she had informed me that she was going to have a press meeting more likely tomorrow and how the mirror wanted to speak with me in she would be informing him later that I seem to be okay.

"Charnel, I don't care!" 'Leave me alone like now."

I watched her come closer listening to her tell me to relax when she saw me push away from her deeper into my bed but where was I going to go.

"Listen to me negro, you have bigger issues than that right now… your life could be in a world of shit as we speak and there is no one to blame but your own selfish black ass." Charnel yelled.

I watched her move back place in her hand on her hip saying how she was told not to say nothing but I'm going to tell you for your own good.

"Tell me what?!" I yelled watching her walked toward several other patients checking to see if they were sleep before coming my way.

"Those two little hoes you had in your life has file a rape charge against you."

"That bullsh*t, you were there." I shouted.

I watched her go into her purse.

"Look I got something to show you." Charnel said.

"You know that bullsh*t, they gave me the ass willingly, remember?" I said loudly.

"Look negro." She said while holding her hand on her hip and almost hitting me in the face with medical documents." 'Your sweet little Stacy and her friend, now do you comprehend what I'm telling you!" 'You basically just f*ck your life away and these papers define it." Charnel said angrily.

I watched her get up walking around with tears in her eyes.

"You're nothing but a rapist and you are voice away from the spotlight with her parents and maybe even her family by now." 'Rapist…what do you've to say in how you get your way out of this one?" Charnel kept looking around seeing if anyone had awaken.

There was nothing I could say, the proof was before my face as I thought about my entire life and where I wanted it to go. I had always been so careful to avoid sh*t like this and because of my own ignorance, it was looking me dead in the face as well as Charnel.

"You want to see more." She said with her hand on her hip pushing more document in my face.

I was in some deep sh*t and like Charnel said, I have bigger problems to worry about while she stood looking down on me before she found a folding chair pulling it closer to my bed. I watched her get comfortable saying how there was so much more but somehow that moment the Mayor himself busted through the door without warning. His aggressive demeanor told me what he wanted while looking at Charnel and then me. That moment I watched her stand up asking him

"How are you Mayor?" Charnel ask.

She treated this n*gga like if he was the president or something but he said nothing as she reached out to shake his hand. It was nothing no more than the respect she had for that n*gga as she moved his way.

"Hey, what bring you here?" I ask.

I felt him pushing down on my shoulder like if he wanted to push me directly into the floor through my own bed. Maybe it was spotlight around him as his entourage made their way inside.

"You seem to have a lot on your mind Mayor." I said.

I was surrounded if they came to see me or was they still kissing his black big ass, politics was nothing more than again of exposure and those searching for what we had had. So much fakeness, their presence blinded in with the un-empty bedpans.

"Mr. Pope, how is it going for you…your secretary was telling me that you're getting better?" 'I come to see for myself." Mayor stated.

This game of chess was never ending while listening to all their crap knowing if I ever become Mayor, all these bastards are fired. The door opened once again and it was that funny talking dread head coming my way singing through the crowd like if he owned the place.

"Goodtz mourning mei friendtz" He said loudly.

"What do you want and what're you looking at Mr. Dreadlocks." I ask.

"Itz me Shaba yao medicaul proafessiunal…mei Shaba mei friendtz frum laust nita…remeumba mei maun…thesz aru ya friendtz riught…awh goodz louking friendtz ahe. It'z is tiume toa changz yoa duode pot yeh!"

"Get a way for me, there is no duode pot here." I said loudly while everyone look at my ass.

"Aha mei Shaba I cum to yao coamediune shoz ahei…yoa very funnyz coumedi guye…yoa bei embarezz oaf thei doude huz…it'z isz okai…Shaba professional medicual maon…mei louk unda foe doude pot mei friendtz." He said loudly like if we were all deaf or something.

"Get the hell away from me!" I said even louder.

It was that moment, he shoved his way in closer feeling under my bed, the look in his eyes had told me he found something. The way he brought his hand out with this disgusting look upon his face.

"Nausty maun…yoa shitz too muach agaun mei friendtz…louk aut mei haund frum yao shiut maun."

Everyone looking on my embarrassment.

"You are so unprofessional dread headman, you should have been a comedian" I said.

Everyone wanted to laugh from the way he frown after reaching back under my bed, he was nothing more than disgusting, even worse the way he kept talking about how bad it smell.

"Louk aut thi Popa shiut, itz nausty maun wouldunt yao sai… louk aut thei colurz oaf tha doude poup hei maude."

He kept waving the dual looking rusty looking sh*t pan in everyone was face was just un-call-for, even the Mayor himself turned his head way.

"Shaba hauv to throaw awauy doude pout nouw, yoa ass ruiened it." He said loudly.

We watched this clown almost leave until he had returned sitting it on my bed while mumbling to himself shaken his head while writing in his chart. That he place back in its metal holder attached to my bed.

"I very sorry for this clown behavior." I said.

The sight of him making his way toward others patients while glancing at me shaking his head while everyone stood in silence. The sight of him walking way was nothing more than a relief seeing how everyone tried to act as if nothing happen. But the smell alone still lingered while the thought of my bare ass was completely out with nothing beneath me.

"This place has the worst service ever." I said.

I'm not the only one who thought that right now, this country was becoming a haven for the worst kind but if America wasn't giving opportunity than fore sure this country open up its doors.

"This place is living proof why we don't need all these foreigners and look at some of these patients with one foot in the graves." 'Someone is going to pay for this." I said.

"This isn't a joking matter." Mayor said.

That moment the alarm caused us to look around wondering where is the rushing Medical Staff, there was no one. That dread head had return checking monitors but everyone had waking up, it was Mr. Jones who gotten up.

"Help!" He kept yelling.

We could see this man struggling just to stand up coughing the entire time grabbing anything within reach.

"That man has one foot in the grave with his bony wrinkle body, did anyone hear him yelling?" I ask.

"Someone heard him." Someone said.

"What the hell." It was all I could say when that same dread head had walked in singing like if it was nothing while smiling at us.

He stood looking at this man before getting his chart reading it while monitors was sounding like alarm fighting for his life. We watch him die while this Dread Head look our way before checking this man out like if he done something important. We saw no CPR or anything.

"It may have brought this man back to life…this place really suck." I said.

We could hear other patients getting but it didn't take a rocket to figure it out while looking at him do what he could to quiet them down. He even ejected some of them with whatever he had on him before shoving it back in his pants pocket. Not once did we see him use new needle, it silence everyone as he return back to the old wrinkle grey hair toothless man that just died.

"Hea wea giuve thea beest oaf caur aut mei familz medicual estuablizment oaf Heuven Medicual Fazculity…thez oul maun itz wiuth Guodz iun thez Heuven nouw aund thez others aure inz auh very goud sleup nouw." He said.

We could do nothing but look at this psychopath now covering up the old man while singing none stop about Heaven and Jesus and God.

"Hey where is your Medical Staff!" I yelled

We watched him stop dead in his track coming my way raising up the covers smiling at me before standing over me.

"Mei…Shaba itz veri buisy maon yulz sei…buot mei Shaba hauve nout furgetz mei goud friendtz yoa…mei Shaba gout juust whut yoal neudtz mei friendtz."

We watched him leave us with this dead body returning with a heavily rusty looking stained bed pan.

"Mei friendtz...nouw youl gout neuw duode punz aund pleuze dunout deustruy thiz goud duode punz...theuy coust muuch muuch biug money...biug dollurs mei friednz butt nouw youl cun doude."

I done what I could to push him away as he place the dead man sh*t pan underneath me.

"Hei wunt bea neudin itz anymou."

"You're one sick dread headed bastard." I yelled.

Everyone around tried to calm me down, it was that moment that two others came thru the door that we couldn't understand. They stood around the dead body looking before someone grab his chart, we could see the older over weight woman looking. They covered him back up before wheeling him out, this placed operated much different anything I ever seen.

"Are you ok?" Charnel ask.

It wasn't her or anyone else, it was this insanity knowing there was a much bigger issue going on with me.

"Mayor what is the real reason you are hear?" I ask.

Silence came about us.

"Mr. Pope you're right, it is time to talk about business now." Mayor said.

He was never a good sight to begin and his hypocritical cronies.

"Mayor, if you are worry about me coming back to work, it want be long." I said.

He stood there for a moment looking at everyone who seem to be in complete silence.

"We have a problem." Mayor said looking around.

Ms. Glasco reach into her binder and pull out a stack of papers handing them to the Mayor as he stood waiting to receive them. It was that moment he look at me before giving them to me when I was trying to readjust myself from this stinky bed,

Relax." Mayor said.

I gotten this nasty taste in my mouth while feeling strength less until Charnel came helping me to stand up looking at the papers in my hand that he insisted that I read and signed.

"You want my resignation?" I said.

This blotted over weight big belly was serious.

"Mayor you can't be serious." I said.

He stood shaking his head up and down as if I was going to accept this bullsh*t.

"This is the best for all of us that you leave quietly before you make it any more worse then what it already is right now." I said.

The sight of everyone standing around looking on like if I was a King being stripped of his Kingdom is what this felt like while Charnel looking on in silence.

"Listen here, you were in hot water these last couples of days and we were on the verge of losing a large federal grant worth million…what you done was more than un-call for and the media alone would've love to run the story of it top Officials being accused of rap." 'My reputation was on the line.

"You said, meaning what Mayor?"

"I want you to sign that resignation and simply walk away. Mayor said.

I stood there wanting to know more.

"If you're worried about your secretary, im sure with her good work habits that we would like to keep her on." Mayor said.

He reach into his coat pocket and hand me an ink pen.

"I can make it look like you have some medical issues with a farewell ceremonial." Mayor said.

I'm surprise he didn't mention Charnel stripper days since he was been so sleazy or my rumor investment.

"Mr. Pope, you're no longer needed and this is the end of your political career representing me!" 'You signed this paper and walk away quietly!" Mayor said.

There wasn't much for me to say while accepting the ink pen noticing him smirking knowing this would be the end of me altogether. One simple signature would change my entire life forever from this day forward.

"Your cousin will be leaving as well." Mayor said somewhat laughing.

I stood there looking at him wondering how in the hell did he know that.

"Signed the dam papers!" Mayor yell after I had taking a seat noticing him looking toward the door that flew open.

The sight of someone closing it.

"Mayor, what happened if I don't sign?" I said.

He stood there rubbing his head looking down while slightly moving that big body of his without taking a step in any direction.

"Listen here, we just got you out of more sh*t then you can climb out of and it costing more money than you would have made in years of employment." 'This county don't need Mr. Harris or your little girlfriend dad walking in starting a war with us that we have no way of winning." 'We settle with him for 75.000 dollars and giving him fulltime employment." 'Your little white girlfriends who lives with her grandmother cost us the 250.000." Mayor said.

That moment Ms. Glasco stood there smiling.

"Signed it and moved on with your life because you're just cost this county more than what you're worth. The mayor said loudly.

This is insanity knowing I gambled everyday with my investment and this job was the same.

"Sir, I have one question before I signed this."

"What is it?" mayor shouted.

"Do you know how I ended up in this dump?" I ask.

He looked at as if he wanted to hit me that very second.

"You don't remember this place?" Mayor ask.

"No, I don't." I replied.

"This was one of your decision and I wanted to override it but I didn't about two years ago...Meaning, we would have taken over this private Medical Facility but im sure they know who you're." 'It was me who transfer you here, hoping you recognize the decision that you made." 'There struggling, even you can see that it's mostly family operated."

Silence came between us that very moment listening to him blurt out.

"Sign it!" Mayor shouted.

I hesitated knowing I needed more time.

"I can only hope that nothing is released concerning those two young ladies you rape." Mayor said.

Those words gave me what I needed to hear looking at Charnel enter the room.

"Are you okay?" Charnel ask.

"Yes, I'm fine." I responded.

"So do you know about what just happen?" I ask.

"Not really just different conversation concerning you." Charnel said with attitude.

It was okay knowing that fat ass mayor wanted my head on a platter knowing I helped him to get reelected plus he is very persistent.

"Charnel, im sorry for what happened between us in the office and I'm sorry that you had to see two girls but you know it wasn't rape.

She stood there looking at me in silence but the moment I started to talk again, she told me to shut the f*ck up.

"You need to get your rest." Charnel said.

"No, you to get me the f*ck out here." I said loudly.

"No, you need to rest just in case the Mayor is serious about the press." Charnel said.

"Do, I look like I'm ready for a press conference?" I said.

"How is your ribs doing?" charnel ask.

I was in some major pain listening to her apologized for what she done, I should've told her to shut the f*ck up like she just told me.

"Charnel. Can you help me?" I ask.

"How?" Charnel ask.

"Have a cab waiting or get ahold of my cousin and park down the street tonight around midnight, this filthy ass place should be quiet by then." I ask.

I watched her leave,

"Bye." I responded.

Good luck, with my wishful thinking, she told me that it would be easier for her to wait outside for me, she left shaking that big booty out the door for the world to see as the night had come. But to my surprise it wasn't Charnel but her ghetto ass friend who I assumed had no love for me as I was at a loss for words listening to her mouth the entire time. This was going to be a very long ride as she told me how she would've cut me on the spot but my friend love your smelly underwear.

"Hey, you get your check this month." I asked.

"Yea negro…I got it, do you want to add to it or something…you know a bitch can always use some more money…so where is it at since you asking and all."

The sight of her ghetto ass was the reason why this country is never going to improve from her dropping one after another fatherless baby. She was the parasite on our infustructure ruining our economy from her first breath as we continue in her beater of a car.

Chapter 10

Stacy

That night that I had gotten home, their was this strange feeling that I wasn't alone just before I made myself a drink to before going to sleep. The next several days had brought on the weekend, it was a time to check my investments but when I had gotten home. I found myself walking from room to room with my 9mm like if I was ready to blow something away any second. My heart beated none stop the entire time as I expected something to happen.

"What the f*ck." I yelled.

It was that moment, she screamed her loudest waking up the neighborhood from the sight of my gun aimed at her.

"It me, Stacy…what the hell are you doing pointing that at me." She yelled.

It was that moment I calm down looking at her completely naked in my bed causing me to put my gun away.

"I wanted to surprise you daddy." Stacy said.

That second she rushed me, her naked body covered me while apologizing for not telling me that she was coming over. Her none stop kissing felt so good but wrong at the same time.

"Stacy you need to put yur cloths on and get dress like now." I told her while holding my ribs.

"Baby, we one everything you ask daddy." Stacy said.

I physically push her away from me just too even get a word in hoping that she actually understood…she kept getting closer.

"Baby, you know I love you daddy and I would never do anything to hurt you. Stacy kept saying.

"Stacy you shouldn't be here, do you want to go to prison for fraud and I'll be going with you for master plaining it." "Shit, I'm lucky that I'm not in jail right now listening to her saying how she was never going to let that happen.

"Daddy, you know I love you and only you right now."

"Stacy please get dress like now before Charnel comes here like she did last time and from this moment on, we have to distance our relationship for a while." I said.

We stood looking at each other while she countered everything I kept telling her.

"Okay daddy, we can just be friends and I'll be getting my money soon and give you your portion ok daddy." Stacy said repeatedly.

I could do nothing but agree knowing this was going to get her dress and out of here while she moved toward her scattered cloths. I should've just left the room but the sight of her booty wobbling with her movement was nothing more than perfection. So curvy knowing she knew I was looking, it was that moment Stacy started giving me a show. She knew I couldn't resist and it would be hard for me to say no especially the way she kept bending that ass over. Stacy had my complete attention making it very difficult for me to think clearly.

"You need to stop like now Stacy." I said repeatedly but it had done no good.

She kept pressing her naked breast upon me the more I pushed her away but her soft lips on my neck had become my weakness.

"I want to feel you deep inside me just one last time and I promise I will leave you alone, it's a woman need daddy." Stacy said softly.

I should've just stop it no matter how she was making me feel right now but my will power had weaken from her soft caressing touch. I felt her kissing all down my chest while moaning was enticing me even more when I tried pushing her away.

"Stacy you need to stop and I need to get away from you." I said.

"Just a little daddy, what is it going to hurt now, I'm already here so just relax and let it happen baby." Stacy said.

I felt her kissing on my zipper the moment she pulled me onto my bed, this was nothing but trouble but it was hard for me to resist. She was doing all that I like from beginning to end until I was inside her, we never had just sex…that was forbidden. Stacy made sure we made love to each other as I found it hard to resist holding back as I let one go inside her.

"That was amazing daddy, you filled a b*tch up good daddy." Stacy said.

She had gotten what she wanted as I watched her get dress slowly and walked her out the back door.

"So we are just friend's from now on right daddy." Stacy said in a soft sexy tone of voice.

Something told me to let things lay low for a minute and not to cross that line of no returned with her and somehow this was going to come back to bite me in my ass sooner than I think. I could only hope that I'm wrong for having such a thought as ended up drinking when I heard the doorbell ringing, I wondered who the hell it could be right now until I actually saw the door handle moving. Before I could even get back upstairs to get my 9mil, the door had been forced open like if the police was entering but it wasn't.

Chapter 11

Gangsters Death

My eyes had gotten bigger when I saw it was my cousin.

"Hey, cousin…put some clothes on like now I'm not trying to see nothing hanging or your bare ass out like that but I got something for you my nigga!"

The sight of 10 gee looking me dead in the face the moment he toss it my way saying.

"Clothes cousin clothes, please cousins…that too much for my eyes to be looking at right now!"

I was still surprise to even see this fool standing here just making his way into my home alone with this shady deal that I know nothing about but at least the niggas was honest.

"What is this?" I said.

"First cousin, wrap something around yoa ass please." My cousin said once more.

"No, you tell me what the f*ck is this first?" I said.

"Cousin, it all there and its concerning Boy Willie."

I stood there looking at this fool knowing now what was going on but I wanted to hear it from his loud mouth.

"Well?" I responded while watching him stand there smiling.

"What is so funny, maybe I want to smile cousin…why are you so happy and shit?" I ask.

"It's done cousin." He said calmly.

Something wasn't right about my cousin, there was something more he wanted to say…normally my cousin was straight forward.

"What've you done Mr. Bowen is all I wanted to know." I said.

"That ten gees you got and you need to add five more to that." He said loudly.

"Why?!" I ask.

"Ok, if you must know cousin…I do my best to keep you out of the shit because of your political life style and all but Boy Willie got pop at his baby moma house over some dumbshit!"

"So, what does Boy Willie got to do with me Mr. Bowen?"

"It's good you ask that cousin because he has a lot to do with you right now cousin." He said.

I stood here with my d*ck and balls swinging from side to side just to see what he was going to say.

"Well cousin, when they took him, they search his crazy b*tch house for weapons and shit like that!" 'Big Nose Freddy won't see a dime what you got from him and you've to know how he didn't have it at the stash house child care center like he should've." 'They found every bit of it at his baby momma house and you don't want to be in Big Nose Freddy debt, that n*gga comes with too much interest and it piles up like shit in an outhouse. 'You can't even get him to see a brighter light when it's comes to his paper.

Dam, I yelled.

"I told you that n*gga was foul."

I thought to myself about what to do next, this n*gga might get some time but he could still be powerful from inside. I could hear my cousin say how, we better hope his bitch ass don't snitch and give up our entire operation enable to save his own black crusty ass. I was at a loss on the street and I had a lot to lose if he opens his mouth.

"You know I can get Two Time to take care of him for us while he is in the lock up."

I could do nothing but look at him and take a moment to think before having someone sleeping for nothing. But there was a dead line to think about while wondering how much is the financial cost.

"How much does it takes to off Boy Willie?" I ask.

"What you say cousin?" Mr. Bowen ask.

"You heard me, how much?" I ask.

"10 to 15 G's…niggas are broke these day cousin and looking for a proper payday." My cousin replied.

"Shit, I could pop the fool myself for that price" I said.

My cousin just look at me, he wanted to know if I wanted it done or not, his mouth never seem to stop moving. He told me how the system got him now and he is not the average n*gga walking around on the street free anymore. My cousin had a way of putting words knowing back in the day, both of them had beef with each other causing me to get involve bringing peace between them. The way my cousin kept talking, it was like he want Boy Willie sleeping forever and soon but I like the way he kept me out of shit like this.

"I got this cousin."

He had taking my money saying how if it cost more, he will put up the 5 G' now but wanted to be reimbursed, it wasn't the first time.

"That what im talking about cousin!" Mr. Bowen said.

I watched him walked away with my money but it was alright, that's alright because Boy Willie wasn't going to be breathing any more. It sad because I never had that many problems with him but all niggas f*ck up from time to time. The thought of what he may have told his baby moma had me a little bothered as I wonder what he may have told her about the operation. But then again, maybe he said nothing and it's just my way of thinking, but I know niggas and how they be running their mouth like b*tches these days.

The thought of another 10 G's be adding up knowing im going to have to play this one by ear more than anything.

Chapter 12

Mr. Harris-Vice Mayor

It was long before I gotten myself together, my nuts has been hanging freely to long now. Several more days pass me before I ended back at work standing before the Mayor himself who doesn't seem to be so happy with my presence from the look in his eyes. His expression told me that alone knowing I was walking a tight rope with this man. I could only hope that I don't slip or I was a for sure goner while waiting to see if he was going to offer me a seat.

This fat ass of a big body was really pushing my luck, he was a man of power within this building but he had nothing past these walls like I do. One phone can have this man pushing up daisy before he even knew what happen to him. But this man was like an uncle to me if not family altogether because we've such a long history. It's was really the only thing that was keeping him from feeling the inside of a casket.

Ms. Glasco had come inside alone with Charnel was changing every time I saw her but she being following in their shadows. It would soon be a thing of the past as I missed her painted on cloths and pony tails that she use to wear to work. It was also something of the past with her but I like her knew professional look, it was like if she had become one of them. The sight of those paper had been slide my way once again as this seem like it had become some game between the Mayor and myself.

His words meant nothing to me, he didn't have his army of ass kissers around him right now. But, so many passed by his office to see what was going on as I stood towering over him like a prize fighter but in reality. I was no match for a big man his size, my experience was base off of loving and nothing more and beneath all that fat, he had to have mad insane crazy strength.

"Mr. Pope, you're done in this business." He shouted like if it impress me or something.

The sight of one of his f*ck buddy had passed by looking all concerned like if he wanted to hear everything going on between us. It was that moment I watched Charnel forcing him to move on but not so much with words. She had this evil crazy look in her eyes that even gave me a form of freight only because I know she was nuts. She should've been my main protection. There wasn't much for me to do here as I had taking a seat not caring what this blab of shit thought eight now. I had enough of his childish treatment and the more he told me to get up the more I ignored him.

"Now you listen here Mayor, what I done wasn't wrong but I can't change the past, it being taking care of and I owed you big on this one." *'We both know this but you want me to sign my resignation away like if im nothing, my career is in your shadow but it want always be there of doing stuff you don't want to like cutting ribbons or speaking at school or just being in public sight." I said.*

"You're done." Mayor said.

"If you want me out then go thru the proper channels and remove me!" I said.

The sight of his new Vice Mayor said nothing as I walked out looking at him and his secretary looking on as I wanted to go to my office but I left it alone.

"I'll be back tomorrow to assume my job and I want my office just the way I left it." I said calmly.

I think no one could believe what just happen, that tub of monkey shit has always treated me like some child and it was a surprise to him that I fought back. The sight of Mr. Harris had appeared from the distance moving closer to me with each step. If this would have been a western movie. There would only been one man standing once the gun stop blazing, maybe he would've been the last man standing since he had more to fight for.

I had been messing with his daughter but at least he gotten full time employment out of it alone with a small account. I watched him bald up his fist the closer we were getting, this wasn't good but in reality, he had every perfect right in my eyes. It had only taking a moment before we were face to face with each other, maybe it was better that he was here than somewhere else where he could blind side me with anger and my possible death.

"Hi and how're you." My first word to him.

I could see that this man had a lot on his mind.

"Would you like to talk?" I ask.

This wasn't going to be easy, he had been compensated but sometimes that not enough for the anger that lived within this man right now.

"We need to talk Mr. Harris." I said.

He just stood there until I whispered in his ear to just follow me, it had taking him a moment to follow me s we pass the Mayor and his b*tch f*ck buddy.

"Just keep moving Mr. Harris." I said.

Charnel kept looking his way smiling knowing she was the one that had relax him to appoint of not making a big unnecessary scene. The press was always around somehow and somewhere, we had arrived outside in the patio area but before I could get the area completely cleared. I found myself on the ground from a cheap shot the moment I turned round to see if he was ok. The way he kept kicking me his hardest even while Charnel had gotten in front of him.

There wasn't much I could do but cover up my rib area that was still in pain, even with the medication that I had been taking. I don't know what had happen but the moment he kicked me right in the head had sent me into another world or something. I had awaken to the sound of something weird.

"Yoa funni like Shaba luvz the furi stufa ya knowa mei Shaba getz all womuz prugnunts…like Shaba bei wut yoa coul bubae duuda ya knu!" 'Escupa latz feu duys yua!"

How in the hell did I end up back in this dump listening to this none talking dread head foreigner babbling on about nothing. He need to build a breath freshener in his mouth but I had to ask him to just stop talking please. He just looked at me but it was that moment he wipe that dumb as facial expressing from his face.

"Hey we have city fire code." *I said loudly.* **"No ciuty fiure cuode here, only me Shaba.**

I watched him pull something from underneath his shirt before placing it back throwing his hand up afterward.

"Seiz mauster keuy." *He said.*

I had no idea what he just showed me or what it even meant as he walked away showing me those heavy yellow stained teeth's in his mouth.

"What an idiot." *I said.*

It was that moment he stop dead in his tracks looking back but he said nothing in returned before completely leaving. The door had swung open minutes later.

"Shaba is no iduiot maun…wut mei dou ta yua!"

I could do nothing but listen to what he had to say about how this country had made his family dream come true. He told me how it was them that are doing something great with their lives and how it is a blessing to be taking great care of peoples with what they have. But it was me who denied them the funding to make this place better than what it was. This dread head had a lot on his mind as he told me that they are learning to depend on themselves and no one else because they're the n*ggers to this country.

There was nothing I could say but watch him leave after venting, the best part of his entire conversation was that he was out of my sight. The sight of several other walking in doing what they could to the other patients had me wondering about their presence. How could we improve if we have every leach knowing coming up out there filthy environment and leaching off of our economy one after another. I needed some fresh air from this foul smelly room, the sight of a rob hanging near of this night mare of a place.

There hasn't been not one staff member that doesn't look as if they were homeless before being drag in here and giving job of some sort. This place should be condemn causing me to wonder how they even operate but the sight of guard patrolling the hallway was something I didn't need to see. Maybe it was his job to make sure that no one escape until this place received their money is all I could come up with. I gotten somewhat down the hallway when I had run directly into a Liberation Prison Guard looking directly at me.

There wasn't much we said to each other as I walked right by him, it made me wonder if this dump is where they brought the injured prisoners or something. Maybe they really did need the funding while hearing the sound of Shaba voice in my ears the sound of the wind blowing felt so god that I had taking a seat underneath this big tree. I must to have fallen asleep until morning looking up at my cousin and some staff member looking down at me.

"Hey can I have a moment with my cousin." He ask.

I watch the medical staff member leave.

"What now Mr. Bowen?" I ask. "It's...Boy Willie, see, here is the problem...the words on the street is that he is dropping dimes on not just you but the entire operation and you it's costing 25 G's to silence him like now before the FBI question him." 'Now... I know he is schedule for general population medical exam. They will be moving them niggas like slave on a plantation for three days by an inside contact.

I stood there looking at him knowing I don't have much of a choice if I'm to move forward and my cousin always been straight with me and if he didn't. It's only a little off the top, every n*gga has to do a little dirt to enhance his saving ability.

"Hey cousin I need an answer about what you want to do and the money complete up front to my contact." 'I tell you who he is but you don't need that info right now, the least you know is the better for you in the long run."

He was right as I don't need to know as he stood there looking at me.

*"Ok, Mr. Bowen, let make it happen as I left only to returned with another 15 G's, that n*gga was costing me but it was nothing compared to what I had planned."*

"Hey cousin, it's Big Nose Freddy doing the hit." I ask.

I had to know if it was him because this n*gga got polices and judges on his payroll and the n*gga has his own sanitation department and cemetery. My cousin just stood there looking at me like if I really wanted to know.

"Okay, never mind Mr. Bowen." I said.

Several more day had pass, it was that morning Charnel had brought me in the new paper saying look what made front page. I had no idea what she was talking about until I seen how it wrote how local Mobster Boy Willie committed suicide doing a medical examination. He hang himself from a bath room water pipe system with his prison jump suit. I ended up one more day in this waste of a dumpsite before I was back in power. If I was mayor my first task would be to bring them up to code knowing they wnt be able to and send them all back to the hole they crawl out of.

Chapter 13

Resignation

My release was nothing more than a blessing to be back at work but there was still some unsolved issue that had to be dealt with. Mr. Harris had been suspended for a few days but I still had my own bone to pick with him, I was told that he was pending even more discipline action once he returned to work. I had a different type of justice to give to him since I came at him like a man and he had taking a cheap shot at me but he taking it too far.

It was that moment Charnel had walked inside with a cup of coffee in her hand as she handed it to me after taking my drink from my hand.

"What is this crap and its straight black, is there any creamer or sugar in it and when do you decide what I drink." *As I sat it down looking at her.*

"You've a meeting with the Mayor like now, he is waiting for you." *Charnel said.*

We must to have talk for a minutes she told me about all that had happen since I was gone, it wasn't much accept for that bastard of a kid.

"The mayor should've just let him go back home and it be done with but he had his reason on the big set I believe Charnel.

"You need to finish your coffee and then we can leave." *Charnel said.*

The moment we started past to his office, all eyes on me listen to Charnel tell me how she couldn't go any farther. I had taking a seat while looking at his big body.

"Who told you to sit?" *Mayor Phillips yelled.* **"So you want to stand or something."** *I ask.*

He said nothing maybe he realized that I could take his worthless life with a phone call from my own office and I allowed him to control this conversation.

"Mr. Pope, it's been two days now." *Mayor said.*

"Yes it has, I think."

"So have you decided yet?" *Mayor ask.*

He slid my resignation papers toward me as I done nothing but look at him and his secretary as I have had enough of him and now her as well. The thought of her even been here made no sense to me right now.

"So, what is your decision Mr." *Mayor ask.*

I had taking the papers holding them saying nothing at first.

"Listen here Mayor, you want me to resigned, well sir…it's not going to happen as long as I can prevent it today or tomorrow as we've had this talk before and you are still not accepting what I have told you. I intend to finished this term and maybe even run for Mayor next time around two years from now and if you or anyone else have a problem with it. Then I expect to be voted out of my *seat."*

It was that moment I laid it back on the table pushing it toward him looking at Ms. Glasco frown on what she just witness. He had done nothing but cross his arms looking defensively.

"Okay then Mr. Pope…if that how you want to play it from now, I tried to do thi the easy way but you seem to not understand when you've a friend on yur side."

"Do what you've to Mayor and I'll do the same."

"You really want the world to know what you done to those two little underage girls and do you really want to disgrace your family name by being called a pedophile and can you live with that for the rest of your life in prison." **'You know this is not America, we brand child molesters in this country…is that what you want on your face?"** **'Do what is right for yourself and the City of Liberation."**

"I gave you my answer Mayor." I said.

He sat there saying nothing.

"Okay, I'm going to use every inch of my authority and run you out of office, I suggest you get an attorney and prepare to face the charges of child molestation." *Mayor said.*

"Mayor, your threats…does this end our friendship becaue if we're…than I hate to become your enemy and with that Mayor." 'I assumed that meeting of friendship is over."

It was that moment that I had gotten up wishing him a great day before ending up back in my office looking at my bar. It was like, all that alcohol that I invested in had come up missing and no one seem to know nothing about it. I knew I should've taking it with me as some of them will be hard to replace. It was that moment that Charnel had walk in taking a seat.

"You drink too much and this is the wrong time for it as well." Charnel said.

I just looked at her as I taking another drink and maybe she was right but it's not what I wanted to hear, the thought of that crazy Mayor. His threats was nothing more than hot air from his fat meaty old mouth, even he knew that I know it has already been settle. But if he is serious about opening up a case, than I'm done in this business for sure and to do time in our prison is worser than suicide itself.

"Not now Charnel, this is starting be to a horrible day and I need something to calm my nerves right now and you're bringing me down even more right now." I said.

"Talk to me baby." 'I want you to know that I'm here for you in any way possible and that mayor is only bluffing with you but I know…you know that by now."

I sat there looking at her.

"You know with all that has happen, this man is really getting under my skin." I said.

Something about Charnel told me that it was going to be ok as the day ended, several more days pass and I was told by Charnel to watch my drinking today because I had a meeting. I was to be adjourning the Mayor regarding Mr. Whitefield Jr. but I didn't know too much of it accept for what I had been told by Charnel. I know I should've been listening to the news more while I was off since it's been on every station almost daily but I was for sure the Mayor was going to return him as we spoke about. It obvious that he did not and I wasn't prepared for this or had anything to say on it or what was even expected of me.

It had been mention to me by the mayor days ago while having lunch, he made sure that I knew I was to be nothing no more than an observer. This man had so much frustration in his voice, even he knew I was his right hand man and needed to be kept in the political loop. Charnel gotten up following me like if she was my moma or something.

"Are you serious?" Charnel yelled.

She closed my bar door faster than a field n*gga could bite into a cold watermelon on the hottest day.

"Relax woman, have you lost that dam mine of yours or what!" I said.

"Okay…just tell me why you're always drinking is all I want to know!" 'You know that Mayor has it in for you and he is looking for any excuse to get rid of you!' 'All you do is drink from the time you get here until the second you leave and it's nothing but nothing, are you listening to me!"

"Charnel, I'm a little stress right now and this is what I need to take the edge off especially concerning that little rich bastard and I need you to be on myside for once.

*"You want to me to support your on the job drinking…well im the wrong bitch for that and you're only f*cking yourself right now knowing you've a meeting in 15 minutes.*

"Charnel calm down, it's going to be ok, im not going to even be there in so many ways, the mayor basically told me to shut my mouth because I have no voice over his." 'Meaning you need to relax like now. I said hoping she understand every word."

"Whatever, you need to give me that and we need to be leaving to the meeting like now." Charnel said loudly.

I watched her pour it out before walking toward the door telling me how she had a few things to get for the meeting. It was that moment that I taking it upon myself to fix myself another drink before relaxing a little as it didn't go as plan.

Chapter 14

The Meeting

The way everyone starred at me as I concentrated on my balance before sitting down wondering if they could smell what I had been drinking. This was nothing more than a show of power, the topic didn't even sound that important as I found myself laughing within the first ten minutes of them going round in circles it seem. The more water I drank had this negative affect on me more than positive. It was life if I ws getting drunker from it as I focus on my posture.

"Are you ok?" Mayor ask.

"Sir, I'm great, how're you. Well I am feeling little light headed sir…are you sure this is just water?"

I could see everyone looking my way while Charnel bumped my legs when I didn't respond to something else the Mayor had ask. She stared at me none stop while the District Attorney ask the Mayor something about his authority wondering if it was personnel with Mr. Whitfield Jr.

"Why is that District Attorney?"

"Mayor, we feel that you are doing this for popularity and maybe future election votes."

"Really, why not upholding the law that Im sworn to protect." **Mayor responded.**

We watch the District Attorney spread his arm wide open saying something about the law before he concentrated on me and everyone else.

"Mayor, you need to release this kid because you are going to lose all the way around and you can't compete with the Whitfield family plus you seem to be the only one for this, don't you think?"

This was taking all the attention from me as I was beginning to even feel lighter headed than before and this was turning into shouting match back and forth.

"District Attorney, this isn't up for discussion or a vote and as far as me being elected again, I don't need it from some rich little kid." 'Especially a kid who feel he can come into my city and do whatever he feel and not have some remorse over what he done…good or bad but bad is what I see so far." Mayor said calmly.

"We know what he has done Mayor but this is his first offense in this country and if we can just take him home, this will be all over like now… wouldn't you say?"

"District Attorney Mr. Tom Cowen, what would you do if you were me and he slapped one of your cops and not to mention how he fondle several young women underneath there clothing and two of them he was inside of with force. I said

"Mayor, we're aware of what he has done and this was his first offense in this country not to mention that he was drunk and not thinking clearly and wasn't those women…strippers?" District Attorney said.

"So, what would you do if you were me District Attorney?" Mayor ask once again.

He said nothing in response at first.

"Listen I'm sure the kid will apologize to the cop for calling him a black monkey with a badge and I'm sure his dad wouldn't mind compensating the strippers…sorry Mayor…young ladies to help ease their pain and suffering." it's not just me who want this drop but many more who are higher than you…and if you know what is good for you along with all that sits around you, it's best that this end now." District Attorney said.

I watched the mayor just sit there looking around at him while reading a few papers of concern that had been giving to him. This was a stubborn man and not much was going to change his mind once it was made up and there was no one above him. I hate to say it but I've learned from him about sticking to your decision no matter what someone else thinks.

"District Attorney, in the beginning of this mess, it was you who stood by Mr. Whitfield right and even when he called us a country of monkeys…if I remember you said nothing in our response." 'Now didn't you come to this country from america to study law?" 'Now why is that when America is so big or is it the fact that you've have been placed here because of America and is it true that you have a Harvard degree and why would a man like you want to be over here with us monkeys…meaning you been white and all Mr. Cowen" 'It a simple question don't you think?"

Wow is all I can say as I watched the District Attorney body language, he looked speechless without a word to say and he leaned back in his chair.

"One more thing Mr. District Attorney and you don't have to answer it but how much are they paying you to get him out of this land of monkeys back into you beautiful white America land of the chosen free." Mayor ask without smiling.

"Are you accusing me of something Mayor, if you are…make it plain and clear, be a man about yours, isn't that what you peoples say to each other." 'My peeps.

Mayor said nothing in response as he just looked at him none stop after placing the papers on the table that he had been giving earlier. I could tell that he was getting frustrated by the amount of water he had been drinking.

"Vice Mayor Pope, right?" 'There has been a lot of discussion going on here and not once has you voice you're a word on the topic." 'I want to know what you think about this."

"This isn't a debate Mr. District Attorney." Mayor said.

I sat there looking at him, I guess my voice isn't worth anything here and that straight from the horse's mouth.

"Mayor, I would like to hear what he has to say if it is ok with you." District Attorney said.

It was that moment the Mayor looked at me and told me to give my opinion.

"Mr. Cowen, we're a growing country, in fact it was my family who help to set up this country and fought for more land because it was more than us than they expected." 'Now you're a college educated man who still deals with America more than us I believe, why is it that we

gotten this piece of land instead of coastal or why isn't we owning any natural resources, it like we are still field n*ggas picking cotton for the plantation owners in which now is America." "You want Mr. Whitfield Jr back it's understandable but I support the Mayor on this one and if he changes his mind for whatever reason."* "And if he changes his mind than I support him as well, this man broke our laws in the worst way ever and he must be responsible for what he does. I responded.*

"I see where you stand." District Attorney said.*

"I guess I don't have the answer you're looking for but we must all take one step at a time to make both countries progress from year to year." I responded.*

"You have a very strong voice in yur belief." District Attorney said.*

Nothing here was being solved it seem.

"I want to say how we been giving these southern slave states, we're making the best of what we have but it also feels that we have been put back into slavery because we don't totally have our freedom yet. Maybe one day America will remove the chains." I said.*

It was that moment that I had been cut off by the Mayor as I respected his decision of me and said nothing more. I sat listening to the rest of this none sense but it wasn't long after my statement that this meeting had ended. We watched the District Attorney get up making with his way toward me before stopping.

"I could see you going very far in this business, maybe even all the way to the top seat in about 8 years." District Attorney said.*

The sight of the mayor looking on saying nothing at the District Attorney making his way out the door, it was a relief to me as nothing seem to have gotten solve.

"I want to see you after this meeting immediately." Mayor said.*

It didn't matter as I know it was coming, he was going to tell me about my disrespecting tongue again as I watched him continued giving his Uncle Tom smile until everyone was out of sight. I ended up back in my office wanting some of my baby momma but Charnel had this strange bug up her ass. These uppity n*ggas had change her way of thinking, my stripper had been change from a behind the door freak to a woman who now believes in herself. Charnel has become one of them as she had come in and left but it was ok, I had taking several drinks before a little masturbation to help me relax.

My pocket couchie does the same job as the one that walks about plus I know where it's been, I must to have fallen asleep but the slamming of books on my desk had brought me out of my sleep. It really scared me.

"Mayor, how're you is there anything I can do for you sir, is there anything you need." I said.

The sight of him standing in front of me while wiping my eyes and mouth must to have been a sight for him to see.

"Your resignation would be a start." Mayor said.

Before I had a chance to respond, he had pick up my glass and smelling it after shaking it. His eyes gotten bigger as I watched him place it back down as the sight of the bar caught his attention.

"You drink too much and even more at work it seems." Mayor said in a low tone of voice.

"It helps me to relax sir." I said.

"I want this out of here."

"May I ask why Mayor." I said.

"You need help and this is not it, plus is obvious you that you don't know how to control your alcohol consumption." Mayor said.

"Mayor, it is your policy and a drink or two during the day isn't hurting anyone and no one else seems to have a problem with it?" 'Only you sir" I said.

"Do you have a problem with your hearing or do I need to constant repeat myself to you and like I said, I want this out of here ASAP"

He stood there looking at me saying.

"Dam with that policy and like I said I want this out of here like today Vice Mayor."

"Mayor, are you upset about something or are you just having a bad day or is it me altogether."

"No, my day is okay… But from the looks of it, you seem to having a great day." Mayor said.

"Why is that Mayor?" I responded.

He has said nothing back, as he stood there before walking around looking at my pictures on the wall with papers in his hand. I sat here watching him move about my room talking nonstop before stopping at a picture, he told me how I could have it all…only if I learn to play the game, maybe even becoming president just from my family name alone but I had no faith in nothing. Not even the intelligence to know when to walk away with a winning hand. This man knew nothing about me really but he was very judgmental especially said I don't even care about myself. He never mentioned how he had come to me to help when this election and now he thinks he is better than me…peoples are funny and like him, very hypocritical.

"Mayor if I may ask, what is really on your mind, is it about the meeting with the Governor's District Attorney" I ask.

He said nothing while walking away.

"Mr…you really showed your ass today." Mayor said.

"Really and how do you figure sir?" I said.

He told me how he wasn't even shock about what I said because of my drunken behavior.

"Mayor, I was far from drunk." I said.

He was right when he responded saying how I almost lost my head, it was best that I say nothing and let him talk. Maybe the meeting earlier had him upset from the District Attorney, it alone was nothing more than an insult and not once did he apologize. So much had been said, it was like we wasn't even their but then again because we live in Americas shadow. Some peoples can be so rude and it's sad how some will always see us in chains, it was that moment that I watched him place several papers before me.

"You have a week to decide to step down and resign before I pushed these papers forward for prosecution of rape." Mayor said.

I just looked at him as we both knew that if our District Attorney get a hold of these, it wouldn't matter what type of deal was made behind closed doors. My ass will be immediately investigated and I will be in the spotlight. My life would be expose and there was nothing I could do but accept it from this moment on.

"You know, I could marry her and this will be over."

"You could but are you going to marry both of them?" Mayor ask.

He stood there looking at me, it was like he wanted an answer back but I couldn't think of nothing to say although, we could marry as many women as we want in this country. This wasn't America.

"Maybe I will and then what will you have other than hatred for me to resign sir."

"I'm giving you a week young man and then those papers that you now hold are going to be push forward and you keep those because." 'That's your copy" Mayor said.

The sound of his expensive shoes pounded the hard wooden freshly wax floor as he headed towards the door before stopping looking back at me.

"There is a meeting in three days with Mr. Whitfield's Attorney alone with his dad, there is no reason for you to be there or your secretary."

This meeting was done, the second he walked out the door as I wondered if he was either going to even give me the information that was to take place within the meeting…what a bastard.

"Mayor! I will be there." I yelled.

It was that moment he had returned looking at me from the hallway, he didn't even bother to come inside.

"Oh, by the way, there is a trial that day of a rape case and I want you to be there to represent us and also I want some good feedback on the aftermath of the case." 'Do you understand that you're to be there Mr. Vice Mayor?" He said repeatedly.

"Yes sir, I understand." I said.

Chapter 15

Big Shug

So much drama is all I could think once I had gotten home hoping now to relax a little from a hard day's work. My rocking chair was nothing more than a sight to see, as I turned my air-conditioner down the lowest it to go along with the fan blowing directly on me. I felt so tired that I didn't even make myself a drink but luckily I had to sacrifice my stash shoved between the arm rests and pillow. It was better than nothing, my driver made his way into my office.

"Boss, is it okay if he called it a day."

I had to tell him to standby and I'll let him know as I rested another 20 minutes before my cell phone had awaken me.

"Shit it is my cousin." I said loudly.

I hesitated answering it but I knew my cousin wouldn't be calling just to chitchat, he was like me and this had to be about money first. It was one thing that our bloodline had in common if nothing else as he told me to come to Paradise Motel like now. Once I gotten there I couldn't believe what I was looking at, it sickens my stomach to a point that I wanted to throw up everything in my stomach. I had to turn my head and to make it worse, it was one of the American girls.

I never wanted to see her this way, even though I knew she was going to be a problem only because we brought her here by force.

"Who found them was my first questions."

The maid who stood near said nothing but the way she was looking at the owner almost told me what I wanted to know. I could do nothing but look at Big Shug wondering if he had anything to do with this, he was an old school gangster and just as dangerous as being in a pit full of lions and he was known to kill you faster than a rattlesnake bite without warning.

"Hey Mayor." Big Shug said.

I just looked is way shaking my head saying what is this Big Shug.

"It looks like we got a problem Mayor and you know I can't have the police all up in my establishment again, it just don't look right for a business." Big Shug said.

"Big Shug, why didn't you just take care of this yourself and why am I even here looking at this making me an accomplice of your dirt." I ask.

"Mayor, me you go back a long ways and is this one of your girls that you had smuggled over here and now this is your problem." Big Shug said.

I could do nothing but look at him, he was right while wondering what the hell happen.

"You know, im to old of a n*gga too old to be doing time Mayor!" Big Shug said.

I watched him pace back and forth like if you done it himself.

"This was too much Big Shug and more than messy." I said.

But, I rather be here then the media especially once they find out who she is.

"Did anyone see her come in here or her in the area?" I ask.

This young lady was major paper and now she has no more value than a penny. I had taken a look at the maid wondering how loyal she could be orders she have to be put to sleep. I needed some information so I had a talk with my cousin and Big Shug while we had taken a look at her with tears flowing down her eyes over the innocence of Ms. White America death. It had only taken a moment to find out what I needed to know about the maid.

My cousin wanted to know what we were going to do with Miss White America six month old baby, there wasn't much to say but at least a baby was pure white and it wouldn't take long to find it a new home for the right price. Big Shug on the other hand had this crazy look in his eyes, it wasn't just me... my cousin thought the same. Maybe it was the fact that this was his hotel and he had one more time to act up or he was for sure to be living 6 feet deep.

"What do we do Mayor?" Big Shug ask.

I looked at him and the stranger who he brought on knowing we knew nothing about her, this was one of our number one whorehouses. It was nothing more than a profits but the way he was hiring employees that we knew nothing about. He had too much was going on from one day to next and it was nothing more than stupidity.

"I'm asking you Big Shug, why are you playing save a hoe with this maid, tell me you're hitting her on the side."

He stood their saying nothing, I found myself walking back and forth.

"You know p*ssy has no face and all the girls that come here are either ex-convicts, old retired street hookers and new ones that we bring into the game or has no home." I said.

He knew of all the rules and regulations and if we are to exist, it must be nothing no more than a straight line. I watched him stand there like a kid who just done something bad and now the outcome is before his face. I made my way toward the maid just to see where her mind really was, her tears was only a sign of weakness and in this business.

"It can't exist." I said.

We can all hear others passing outside the door knowing this was all I needed, this n*gga has been nothing but trouble and death. I wish I would have never given him this loan for this place but was done is done and now it's time to move forward.

"Hey, are you okay?" I ask the Maid.

She stood there saying nothing back, this wasn't a good sign and my cousin must to have frighten her by the way she was looking at him. I guess I don't blame her, he was another crazy n*gga to be dealing with but he was honest and that was good enough for me. I watched her wipe anyway her tears with the handkerchief that I had given her and told her to go ahead and keep it. I had the find a way to get past her force field to see where her head was or was she willing to play ball.

I could only hope that she was willing to join the team because there was no walking away if she didn't want to sign on with us. The look in her eyes told me that she knew of life and death, there was no in between in situations like this. It was either learning to live with this or accept the death that may come from it but being a lamb around wolves, this alone would make anyone scared and shaking like she was. I never seen this girl and Big Shug really didn't know anything about her, nor did my cousin. T

"Hey, Carla right… listen we are all family here and since you are a new employee, take this money, it's not much only a few hundred dollars." 'Go home and take some time off and relax, in a few days someone will contact you about coming back to work ok, now my understanding you are living at Big Shug Heaven Motel right with your two sisters who are nursing staff right?" 'You're one of us now and I have this gentleman put you and your family, let's say in a three-bedroom apartment near Lake Paradise Park…very nice area…you keep working here and become part of family and we keep your rent very low." 'My promise to you, now go home and get some rest and we would take care this little incident.

It was that moment, we watched her gather her stuff and walked away without saying goodbye.

"Hey cousin, I'm going to keep my word with her but in the meantime…I need you to check her out and if you hear any sign of disloyalty or anything that you don't approve of." 'Get with me instantly, maybe we could be adding three more whores to this hotel."

We all stayed around thinking how to clean up this mess while wondering if we could really trust her or was she going to sing like a tweedy bird the first given opportunity. I had a spoken with Big Shug about calling me the mayor, never knowing why he continue to do it as much as I tell him not to and now because of his stupidity, she knows who I am. Dumb n*ggas will bring you down faster than any other nationality that God created on this earth. I so wanted to leave but this had to be done right, I not just had so much invested in this place but I had my life already planned out.

My cousin told me how that wasn't smart letting her go like that but even I know he was right but we had to give her a chance. There has been enough killing for today and I told him that she could have call the police first. But she didn't only because she know the operation here, that alone told me that she has street smarts and that is something you can't buy. I had taking it upon myself to find out if he still kept in contact with Goldie Locs

"She is state side, maybe around the west coast high mountain area like Oregon the last time I remember Mayor." Big Shug said.

"Can you get ahold of her and have her to contact my cousin, I need some work done."

"When?" Big Shug ask.

"I need her over here faster than you can eat a bucket of greasy fried chicken." I said listen to him laugh afterwards.

"You know she is an addicts and once an addict, always and addict." Big Shug said.

"Yea but she is good at what she does." I said.

It was that moment, the knocking on the door had us on the edge, my heart beated faster than it ever has the louder it had gotten on seconds later.

"Hey, it's me O' Dirty." The Voice yelled.

That moment Big Shug had waked over to the door and before we knew it, this white boy had been forced inside faster than Big Shug could move. The way he had flown right into him, it must to have been a relief to feel something softer than what he appeared to look like. He was a bloody mess from head to toe.

"Hey did any of you genius think of what peoples thought when they saw him being drag in here like this." I said.

I think Big Shug done more damage to him just from the way he grabbed him before throwing him to the floor. The way he had fallen onto the girl, this man gotten way from her like if she was a human disease... that alone told me lot about him. He tried to get to his feet but O' Dirty kicked him in the face while yelling at him to stay down like the dog he ways.

"Boss, here he is." O' Dirty yelled loudly.

He laid there somewhat shaking defensively trying to protect himself.

"Boss, you're going to find this amazing, this cracker as cracker told me that he beat her to death because she as a nigger lover.

We watched him crawl toward Big Shug apologizing as he grabbed his leg, I saw him fly directly toward me from the way Big Shug shook him off before kicking the living shit out of him. It cause me to kick him several times out of anger of this American piece of shit come to our country and do his dirt and like if we were nothing. I had to catch myself when the sight of blood covered my expensive shoes.

"Dam nigga, you ok…it ain't like you was beating the fool."
O'Dirty ask."

I had to catch my breath looking at him and No Neck Blacky standing there stained in blood themselves.

"What the hell did you drag this piece of shit in here for doing working hours?" I asked.

The sight of them looking at Big Shug and the way he threw up his hand like what.

"Really, Big Shug!" I said.

"I'm sorry, he yelled while bleeding from his face, it was that moment I saw Big Shug grab this man and drag him across the floor over." "Look at him her." Big Shug said loudly.

I watched him try to fight back when Big Shug shove his face into her bleeding body, there was so much blood here that it wasn't going to be easy cleaning this up. I watched him been beating the more he tried to pull away but Big Shug was just too strong for him to do anything. The way Big Shug now stood over him while he was trying to catch his breath kicking him every time he thought he had caught his breath. The sight of all of us looking on knowing nothing was coming out of this but another death and it was Mr. White America.

"How did he pay Big Shug and was there anyone else with him."
I ask.

"No, there was no one else with him and he paid top dollar for this one, that how he knew exactly who I was.

The sight of him looking up knowing himself that he wasn't walking away from this no matter how much money he said he had.

"Mr. Bowen, how fast can you get the Butcher over here?" I ask.

The sight of everyone looking on made me feel really uneasy.

"The…Butcher." Big Shug said.

"Yes, do you have a problem with the Butcher, this is your mess Big Shug and his fee is coming from you and I don't care how you come up with it, it can come from your big ass for all I care!" I said.

"Cousin, I can get him over here in an hour easily." Mr. Bowen
said.

Big Shug looked at me and the girl who laid here dead, he knew he had two bodies to pay for and this was coming out of his pockets. It didn't take long for the Butcher to arrive with his utensils and garbage bags.

"Men's we see death so much but life isn't supposed to end like this…remember this picture." I said.

We sat here looking at the way the human body break down until the Butcher arrived, this man was the best in this business. I seen him cut up a body like a hot pizza straight from the oven, he was good at what he does from the way he studied the body like a surgeon avoiding major arteries limiting the blood flow from making more of a mess.

"What a waste." Butcher said.

We watched him look at her private parts like if he just gotten released from prison, the way he shoved his hand into her panties and then smelled his hand instantly.

"She been dead on for a few hours." Butcher said.

I could do nothing but think what a sick bastard watching place plastic all about before breaking out his knives. He went to work after removing her cloths first before cutting her up limb by limb stuffing her in double line trash bags. No matter how many times I saw this happen, it was always sickening to watch.

"Well, im done here but I thought there was another one." Butcher said.

"Shut the f*ck up yelled Blackie No Neck said.

I watched him strike him across the head with his pistol, this white boy had been force to watched the entire time while bleeding none stop from the beating he continue taking. This man had to be in so much pain from the way Big Shug kept cutting his body part with the Butchers toys. Im surprise that he was able to stand.

"You took the life of one of my best whores and you watch what we had to do her all because you say she was a nigger lover, you white bastard." 'Now tell me what should I do to you aside take a few fingers from each hand and shove them down your throat."

We all heard him beg for his life until Big Shut grab the Butcher plier while his boys held, I could hardly look when he reach into his mouth. The sight of his tongue was disgusting as blood pour down his body from the way his tongue was cut. His body squirmed none stop until he had fallen to the floor in pain that I could even imagine holding his own tongue that had been thrown at him.

"Get his ass up." Big Shug yell.

The sight of him running his mouth was going to be his destruction one day but Big Shug love to hear himself talk, not to mention how he was a jokester.

"You've something you want to say Mr. White America?" Big Shug ask him.

This man could do nothing but mumble the entire time, the sound of the music cover any sounds that may have gotten past this room. We watch Big Shug reach for the Butcher knife and begging cutting off his head from the back to the front. I never seen a body move like that ever in my life, it had become hard for his boys to hold him up while my cousin thought it was funny. He laughed and made commits the entire time as none of it was good.

"Satisfied now Butcher." Big Shug gestured.

This was nothing but some sick shit but like I said, Big Shut was an old gangster and this is what he was known for. I wonder if him and this man ever had beef, he would have to sleep before me until judgment day, this n*gga was a real psychopath.

Chapter 16

Little Ms. Mexico

It wasn't long after I ended up back home so much had happen to today that I never expected and I needed something more. A good night sleep right now would be a good to begin with but there was a knock at my door.

"Who in the hell is it!" I yelled.

The moment I open the door, it ws this girl I never seen before, she told me that her name was Monica and that she was sent by Big Shug. I saw her around, she work at the bar and nothing more but I think Big Shug was saving her for something special like a high price call girl. Her innocence kept value in her.

"What can I do for you?" I ask.

"Make you a happy man to start." She responded.

Maybe my day just gotten better as I open the door, this women didn't hesitate to enter, this wasn't like the woman that I thought I knew. Maybe she wasn't as innocents as I thought she were from the way she was acting and not to mention the way she was dress.

"So what can I do for you?" I ask.

"Wrong question boss, the question is what I can do for you." She said in a soft sexy tone of voice.

The sight of her standing there, had rally open my eyes, her full lips had come with a smile like never before, the softness to her voice was like music to my ears. This young woman was so attractive from her long dark hair to the devil red shoes that she had on matching her hooker red skirt. It displayed every curve in her hour glass body, she couldn't have been no older than 25 at the most. It was like she was old enough to know the value between her legs but at the same time young enough to know how to make it work for her.

I could do nothing but be amazed that Big Shug had sent her my way, it also made me wonder why and what was the plan behind it. Maybe he get me all relax and while I'm deep in her ass, this could be away of setting a n*gga up for a hit or do it herself. I wasn't sure but something didn't smell right, it wasn't virgina or the sweat between my balls. I had to figure this one out as I offer her a drink.

"Have a seat pretty." I said.

We had a few drinks while this was my time to figure out why she is here but I couldn't keep my eyes off her full breast or the way her hips spreaded across my couch. Her laughter had giving this place somewhat happiness but the thought of Charnel showing up without notice had placed fared upon this place ruining our sexual vibe. She was the typical crazy hot tempered black woman with a sky rocket personality and revengeful physical attitude if she saw all this good prime ass sitting before me laughing. Charnel was the storm that came without warning and you wanted to avoid at all cost.

"Hey pretty, you know what is weird is that I had this crazy feeling that you never like the ground I walked on." I ask

She had done nothing but smile while taking another drink, the way she crossed her legs after she open them up just enough to give me a glimpse of her silkiness was a sight to see.

"You like poppi, there is rumor that you love the way we pillow talk in bed, is that true poppi." She ask.

"And who told you that and it would be nice to hear you tell me your name." I said. "Ahh poppi, you know my name from the Hotel." She said.

"I want you to tell me." I ask.

"Monica poppi, now does that make you happier?" Monica ask.

I couldn't keep my eyes off her, the sight of her noticing my erection the more she spoke her poppi language in the sexiest voice.

"Hey are we gone get that?"

I could do nothing but ignore my little man but even he knew that it was no way possible that we were going to be along with a woman like this and their going to be some serious pounding. She brought out the weakness in me from the way she scented up my house knowing if Charnel showed up. I would have to hide her, there was no way I could mask her womanly odor, it would linger causing nothing more than an explosion.

"Monica were you going on a picnic or something?" I ask.

"Good you ask Poppi, it for you and do you have a kitchen for me to warm it up poppi?" Monica ask.

She gotten up shaking that big round rump roast of hers giving me a personal show and she knew of it from the way she look back smiling from west to east coast. I wasn't even strapped but for some strange reason I had no fear of her hurting me. Moment later as I scouted the area to see if this was some sort of strange death to come, there was nothing. This woman was alone as she invited me back into the kitchen, the food looked amazing.

"Look what I got for you poppi." Monica said.

I had something for her to and it was only a matter of time before she feel it deep in her ass, we ate like tomorrow didn't exist. It was that moment I took it upon myself to show her why I work so hard knowing this was like the perfect p*ssy palace from the front door to the room that her panties would soon be coming off. Monica seem to more interest in the bath room more than anything now. It was perfect timing as I made a call to see where my crazy other half way.

"Why are you calling me, this is a first…is there some b*tch around you right now or what?" Charnel ask.

"I'm calling to see how my son is doing, is that ok and how're you is all im asking…is that ok with you Charnel?" I ask.

"You want to talk to your son, since you seem to be so concern?" Charnel ask.

I really didn't have much of a choice before she gotten back on the phone talking shit before we hung up.

Women are all f*cking nut insane jealous nut cases, lucky they got a crotch attached to them or they would be worthless. I gotten back with Monica only minutes later having a few more drinks while laughing, my hunger had been satisfied. The sight of her packing up what she had brought over, maybe this was her intentions as I watch her about to leave.

"Hey…lets blaze one up for new friendship sake." I ask.

It was that moment she stop looking at me without saying a word but the sight of my weed stash open her eyes up.

"Okay." Monica said.

Would've been nice of her to speak better but bumping and grinding don't require much communication, she watched me roll a fat one before we blazed it and then another as I made myself another drink.

"You drink too much poppi." Monica said.

She was a blazer.

"That's my girl." I said.

It wouldn't be long now before her panties be touching her ankles if she keeps smoking the way she is as I poured her some more champagnes. She has been here for about an hour now.

"Hey, come over here pretty." I ask

She hesitated but like I said, if it doesn't work than try again as I watched her moved closer to me, she was on cloud nine now and going higher.

"So, tell me why you're really here, are you sent to kill me in my sleep or while you're giving me the Latina piece of heaven."

I listen to her giggle.

"I can show you better than I can tell you poppi."

The way she moved in close exposing those full lips as if she was going to kiss me, I could do nothing but let her do as she please while her hand felt amazing on my leg. It gave me shivers, her soft sexy words was like music as I haven't been with many of her kind but I can certainly understand why their populating this world. This was only a taste of what she had to offer of her sexual nature and she was going to get the fat one bust deep in her mushy-mushy gushy if she keeps this up. There may be a half breed coming into world in about 9 months knowing from the way she look, there is some good stuff down there. It must be magical because my little man wanted to disappear inside of it.

"So are you ready for a night of loving?" Monica ask.

Her un-resistible neck had just gotten the green light, it was going to start there as she pulled the back of my head into her. Her moans blended in with her native language becoming the medicine a n*gga needed. Her strength empowered what was in me, she excited my little man with her intense touch. Monica was only showing me what was yet to come.

Her large breast so wanted to breath from the thin layer clothing as my lips found them, they ere so soft, if I was a baby…there would be no need to complain, if her rip firm melons is what kept me alive. This women was not into long kisses from the way she kept pushing me from her as I watched her slowly move away. She guided my hand to her blouse, it was that moment…she wanted me to unbutton her shirt exposing her fully.

"Wow, what a view Monica." I said.

This was nothing more than eye candy and I wanted to explore every delicious taste of she had to offer.

"I may have to see a dentist after this candy factory." I said

Monica could do nothing but laugh while I felt her unzipping my pants until she had my little man out like her breast, there was no way that this was going to be a onetime sexual affair. It had taking us a moment before I watched her stand up.

"Remove it sexy, remove it. I said.

I would have paid for this show not to mention the way she moved in slow kissing me with those spicy full lips but it was nothing compared to when I felt what made her a woman. There was nothing negative to say about the stuff she was born with as I busted so deep inside of her, this wasn't just a f*ck. Monica had shown me the art of love making until I heard my door bell ringing like a fire alarm.

*"What the f*ck, who in the hell is at my door right now." I yelled.*

I had no choice but to go down and see who it was as I rack one in the barrel, this better be an emergency or someone is going to die.

"Hey, do you have a minute and can I come in." Mayor said politely.

I open the door as he made his way inside holding the n*gga killer.

"You expecting death or something to knock on your door?" Mayor ask.

"Maybe, what can I do for you and why at my home, this better be more than important Mayor!" "So much fire power, can we leave the door open?" Mayor ask."

"No." I said.

I shut the door after taking a quick look outside just to make sure he was alone.

"What can I do for you Mayor, is there anything I could get you." I ask.

The sight of him standing there was better than my baby moma I guess as he caught a glimpse of Monica walking to the bathroom in her devil red panties and bra. The way he stood looking at her while she asked me if she could shower, it was like if he hasn't seen p*ssy that young in a long while, maybe he was used to seeing his wife old hairy grey bush.

"I didn't know you had the company of lady friend, she is very pretty…I see." Mayor said.

"Hey…Mayor, if you want some of that, im sure I could hook it up for you like right now…this house has plenty of rooms, use can even chose if you like sir." I said

"Oh no, my wife is at home waiting for me, she is the only woman for me." He somewhat shouted.

"Okay, im sorry but the way you was looking at her was like if you could just go and ram you d*ck up in her like right now Mayor." I said.

He had said nothing but stood there but every time Monica cross our path, his eyes was glue to her ass like if she ws the only woman alive. It was that moment that I laid the sawed off down on the table, the sight of it made him ask me if it ws needed.

"Mayor, well you know what we represent and the often death threats that comes our way, you can never be too sure these days."

He stood there looking at it before telling me that, there is no reason for me to be at the meeting tomorrow saying how Charnel is going to be there with Ms. Glasco taking notes only. I watched him look toward the way that Monica had been going back and forth.

"Monica, come down for a minute." I yelled.

She had said something back but I asked her again in a different way, she recognized the sound from the whores she seen me deal with.

"Monica, I want you to meet the Mayor of the City."

She stood there without words, as I pushed her toward him to see him just stand there looking at her fully expose breast and perfecting round ass you just want to f*ck until it becomes impossible.

"Mayor would you like to really get to know the real inside of Monica, I'm sure with a little persuasion she will be more than happy to feel the long part of you." I said.

I had taking my finger aiming it like a gun while pulling my finger back the minute he froze like if he gotten caught by his wife before pounding something.

"Busta ass n*gga." I said while watching him leave.

That n*gga is going to get a surprise of his life tomorrow morning, im surprise that he came by just to tell me that. Monica had went back upstairs upset I guess.

"Hey what are you doing?" I ask. "You treat me like a hotel whore, I'm not a whore and I was liken you!"

I said nothing as she kept talking shit none stop like she was special or something, this b*tch wasn't even a normal how walking the street. It was that moment that reality had set in, I gotten her mind al twisted from the way I treated her like if she was a date or something.

"Hey, who told you to get dress?" I asked loudly.

She had done nothing but ignored me like if she someone with an opinion, it was that moment I had to check her. the way she scream when I grabbed her by the back of her neck and slammed her into the wall, she fell but she gotten up fighting back.

"Yea b*tch that how a nigga like it!"

I grabbed her once more after busting into her face and ripped off her clothes until they hung from her body exposing those full melons. Monica fought back the best she could but nothing was going to stop me from rushing back deep inside her.

"That it, relax and take it like the whore you are b*tch, this could've been a wonderful relationship but you had to ruin a good thing." I continue talking to her.

This whore was like a wild mustang but when she decided to fight no more, she had been broken as I drag her from my bed into the hallway.

"Don't move and inch or you want be moving at all b*tch."

I found myself waiting nearly an hour until Big Shug showed up with 2 of his whore and hoods to take her away, he wasn't happy but at least he understood as I watch them get her dress.

"I suggested that you make her a profit."

It was his call, she had been broken and when that happens, there is nothing left but to fill her with dope and watch the money pile up from her destiny on her back.

Chapter 17

Charnel Insane Jealousy

"Hey…wake up, you been drinking too much again she said…get up now." Charnel said

It was that moment she had help me to get up, I felt her dragging me into the shower, the water was freezing cold to appoint I wanted to called her a b*tch. I could hear her telling me everything that I had to do today while I done my best to keep cleaning myself like she was doing only moments ago.

"Who was she?" Charnel ask.

But before I could say anything, she shove some red panties into my mouth while I was still taking the coldest shower ever in history.

*"I want you to stay the hell away from me from this point on and you can f*ck all the b*tches you want from now on and she was on her period…you really are one nasty bastard."*

I watched her shaking while tears rolled down her face and within the blink of an eye, she had slapped me so hard I started pissing. When I had gotten out I went down stairs to see her sitting with a drink in her hand.

"Don't say nothing, we'll deal with this later because I've a meeting and you've to be in court this morning for the next several hours.

There wasn't much I could say, she had removed all my bedding and begun washing it and in between she fix me a little something to eat. Charnel was always good for taking care of me no matter what I done to her, she has always been her doing the thing that a wife would due for her husband.

"You know I started to throw your sheets from whichever nasty b*tch you were f*cking left a bloody mess but it wasn't mines to trash." Charnel aid angrily.

The sight of her holding over 400 dollars cash in her hand after telling me that she had taking it for cleaning not just my filthy ass up but also cleaning behind the nasty bitch that was here. I had said nothing, it was hers too kept along with whatever else she wanted right now knowing I wasn't about to get into a shouting match with her right now plus I don't know what she done with my gun. Charnel had done what she could before leaving as I told her that I now had it under control of making the court appearance. The moment she had left, the sight of my bar look pretty appetizing as I made myself a quick drink one after another while relaxing in my chair.

The sight of my clock by the time I had gotten up was now past 12 o clock, what the f*ck is all I could say. The mayor was going to shit bricks when he find out that I didn't attend that stupid court date. I hd gotten up calling Charnel and informing her that I wasn't coming in due to medical reasons but it just didn't end with one day. The next few days as well only to find my 9mm in the trash, that stripper really had some deep mental issues.

If she only knew the value of a weapon like this, she wouldn't be as stupid but then again…Charnel is a woman, making her intelligence level base around her bloody time of the month I guess. That following Thursday, I had shown up for work, my first meeting was with the Mayor as it didn't go the way I wanted. Charnel had filled me in on everything that was going on, although I could tell that she wasn't happy with me right now either. It was ok with her, im always on her bad side in one way or the other somehow.

I had taken little time to relax after pouring myself a quick one, the mayor kind of stayed on my mind in the worse way. This man really had it out for me, even the way he told me somewhat of the meeting wasn't even good. He wasted my time more than ever as I had to listen to his theory on big government. He was so full of shit and how he told me of Whitfield Jr. had gotten sentence to 30 days and he is subject to public slashing before being released back to America.

Maybe the mayor wasn't all bad as he had a strict policy on crime and harsh punishment, I could only imagine what he would do to me if he gotten the chance. I myself had enough of his hot air about how he takes the time to travel to University and Public School and even with the military. He was nothing but a horney bullshit con artist and it's sad how it taking me this long to see right through him. I had fix myself another cola and rum Until Charnel had walk in ruining my relax time.

"Hey…really, why are you drinking so early and you know how the Mayor told you to get this out of here like days ago." Charnel somewhat yelled.

"You need to worry about taking notes and making coffee, you're nothing more than a secretary Charnel and you need to learn to stay in your lane."

She stood there looking at me saying how she has never made me a cup of coffee and she does more than secretary does when it come to my black ignorant ass.

"So what are you going to do tomorrow, the mayor isn't joking with you and he will pushed those paper forward."

She was right about that, he hold my life in his hand as this n*gga had known about my other life of the streets that I thought he knew nothing about. The sight of Charnel has cross my mind that she maybe his informant or something. Ms. Glasco did take her under her belt and shown her the entire job, she even now dress like the rest of these office hookers. Charnel did know of my business on the street but why would she cross me like that over job like this. This paycheck was nothing more than a joke compared to what I give her when the money is flowing.

"So what are you going to do?" Charnel ask once more. "I take care of that uppity negro, time itself will be his enemy." I said.

The sight of her saying nothing in response had me somewhat worried from what I said while being un-sure whose teams she is really on now. We sat here a bit longer but by the end of the day, we had both gotten our days wrong. The office would be close that following Friday.

Chapter 18

Sheriff Office

"Good morning Mayor is all I hear." **As I entered this building of sadness.**

The next several days passed, Ms. Glasco who still seems to be very distant to me, I guess her heart is still sad over the tragedy but it's understandable about the grief that is upon this place of business.

"How're you today." I ask.

She looked at me like if she never seen me before.

"I'm okay." She responded. "You know we could be on a first names basis or we could keep it professional. I stated.

Later on that week, I had invited her into my office.

"Well, Ms. Glasco, I know that this is very hard for you and I know you want to know why I denied your vacation or at least for now because I feel that you're too important to this operation." 'I feel that you need to be here especially since you seem to know more about the Whitfield case than anyone I know including myself." 'There is so much politics going on that I've been out of the loop for many unknown reasons and I know which your professional ability of high standards level of dedication you done for the former Mayor Phillips." 'But now that he is gone, it's you and I that must maintain the professional level of Excellency for those that have instilled trust in what we represent." 'If you don't mind Ms. Glasco I'll like to take a moment of silence for prayer for his family and his soul as well."

It was that moment, the way she stood looking at me before doing as I ask, it was like she knew that something wasn't right. Maybe she even had an ideal that I was involve as I really didn't know but it was the way she looked at me and how she kept her distance from me knowing we work side-by-side.

"Mrs. Glasco, is there anything I can do for you or your family?" **I asked.**

She stood up there said nothing, her looks alone basically told me to go to hell in a true will come out as I could do nothing but watch her leave never looking back with that ghetto booty just wobbling about the place but I have stopped her before she got completely away.

"Yes Mayor." She said.

"I have one other thing on my mind that I feel should be brought to your attention, the former mayor had authorize you to take personal breaks and unscheduled luncheons whenever you chose to." 'Well…with all that is going on, especially right now." 'I feel that those privileges should be set to aside for the moment, when you feel the need to take lunch" 'Please let me know and I asked this only because, with all that is going on." 'I truly need to know when and where you're just in case something comes up from thin air."

She stood there looking at me, but she never said a word or even attempt to argue over the decision I just made.

"Is that what all men are, because I'm very busy and with everything going on…I've got a little bit behind in my work?" Ms. Glasco said somewhat rude and loudly with aggression in her voice.

I watched her take a few steps turning that big booty my way to me once more before I stopped her.

"Ms. Glasco, there is one other thing… I looked into your personal file and I discovered that you're not really staff and it made me wonder about…how you're able to drive a county vehicle not just on business hours but as if it is your own personal vehicle." 'I have spoken with human resource along with transportation and they are expecting you to turn in those keys and fuel card as well as the city visa." 'We are having a financial problem right now and those cars are to be in the hands of official staff members and I need you to take your ID card and have it reprogram to the data clock. It's only to account for your Secretarial hours, I would want you to experience any type of pay

loss especially now with everything being so hard on all of us from the mayor's death." 'Is there going to be a problem with everything you just heard this Glasco?"

She stood there looking at me with disbelief but she had given me a feeling that I needed to keep her a round just long enough to get this Whitfield incident out the way. This woman had this crazy look in her eyes, that she was going to solve the mayor's death and I didn't need her here any longer snooping around.

"No." Ms. Glasco said before walking away quietly.

I know we both felt this strange energy and amongst us, the moment she was leaving her and Charnel had almost bump into each other, it was like looking at friends become overnight enemies for some strange reason.

"Is or something I can do for you Charnel?"

The way she had come in and sat down looking at me with nothing more than attitude.

"So you finally got the big chair, and how did you get those scratches?" Charnel ask aggressively.

I said nothing back while looking at her studying me up and down as I wondered what was going through her mind. The thought of my girl becoming my enemy wouldn't be good for me nor her and why is she all into my business.

"Charnel, are you okay is there something going on which you that I should know or do you feel that you need some time off." 'You know we are all having a hard time here especially with the mayor's death." I stated.

"So, how does it feel to be sitting in the big chair?" Charnel ask.

This woman wasn't far from Ms. Glasco and all I could hope is that she wasn't going to be trouble.

"Well, you know the story about how the Mayor had a horrifying tragedy along with his family that I've known half of my life." 'He was a very decent man, we both knew that about him." I said.

"Where is your cousin at?" Charnel ask hostilely.

"Charnel, are you sure you're okay today, maybe you need to go home and relax, you seem to be out of place today and I can understand why because we just lost a great man that will be miss but I'm trying

to see this through and if there's anything I can do for you in your time of grief." 'Please let me know."

"First, I'm not a regular employee and don't give me that grief bullshit because of your baby momma, remember the child we had together…The child you wanted me to abort, remember that child… Well, your son made me a mommy and you a daddy and when you find the time… Why don't you come to see how he is doing?"

The sight of her raising her voice becoming very aggressive force me to ask her to keep it professional in this place of business and I told her, that my name is not baby daddy up in here.

"Charnel, let's be adults and you can call me Mayor or Mr. Pope from this point on." I said.

The way she walked away was more than aggressive, even when I told her to send in the next employee or maybe the way I checked her off my list had gotten her upset. It didn't take me long to figure out who was on my chopping list the next several days. The following day I had gotten another surprised visit from the Sheriff, the sight of him approaching from the hallway had my heart beating a little faster than it should have.

"Good afternoon Sheriff, is anything I can do for you?"

"There is Mayor, let's take a little walk if you don't mind… Your patio area should be nice this time of day if you are not too busy?"

"Um, yes I am… Could we do this later Sheriff?"

"It will only take a few minutes of your busy time Mayor, I promise." 'You look like you seen a ghost Mayor."

We talked and chatted for a few minutes, the conversation we had was pretty much about nothing until the topic had come up about my recent ware about.

"So, Sheriff, how has your day been?" I ask

"Well it's funny you say that, it's been pretty crazy, mostly involving this unpredictable death of the Mayor but who wouldn't know more about that then you right, and I never seen such a mess, it was like it was intentionally done to cover up what had been done." 'I'm sure you probably has heard as much as I know about the case right?" Sheriff ask.

"Well Sheriff, I heard the fire destroyed everything, is that true?" I ask.

"You know it's funny about fires Mayor, even when everything burned to the ground, somehow it still has a story to tell." 'You know...I mention that to the fire investigators and we all just got a laugh out of it, because even they agree with me in this line of work but we will all get to the bottom of it, sooner or later" 'There's tales that you and the former mayor go back along ways... would that be true?" Sheriff ask.

I could do nothing but look at him before been asked the question, it was like he was studying me from the way I move to the way I avoid him altogether.

"Well Mayor, is it true or not." Sheriff ask.

"Yes, he saw me grow up, why so many questions Sheriff?"

"It's what I do Mayor."

"So. Sheriff, what have you come up with? If you don't mind me asking."

"Mayor it is pretty routine stuff and now I'm waiting on the Fire Marshall...once their investigation is done." 'I will know what to do from there. Sheriff said with confidence.

"Well S"I was wondering Mayor, what you like to make a statement on behalf of what you might know about this case." Sheriff ask.

"Sheriff, I don't know much about it, just what I heard and to be honest, is mostly from you and of course the news." 'You know how to media can be, they tends to make things more interesting just to get us to listen to them." I said.

"I'm aware of the media Mayor, just a few words about your whereabouts is all that's really needed Mayor, how about today." 'I'm headed back to the office shortly after this...just a small written statement Mayor...few words on the dotted line." Sheriff said.

The way he looked at me, after patting me on the back, it told me that he knew more than what he was saying... this man is making me a suspect.

"Mayor are you coming." Sheriff ask.

"Okay Sheriff," I said.

"When Mayor?" Sheriff ask.

I had told him that I could be down there in less than an hour, he had taken one look at me and with his old wrinkle hands...patted me on the back while smiling. I watched him walk waving bye several times like an old country boy. It wasn't long after that, my every movement was been watched like if I was some criminal or something as I gotten back into my office. I had taken the time to have a drink until Ms. Glasco walked in informing me that the Sheriff was at the station waiting for me.

I could do nothing but look at her while glancing at my watch saying to myself…what the f*ck, she was right as I gotten myself together. They all appeared professional from the front desk to his staff members as so many thoughts pour through my mind, like the friendship between the Former Mayor and the Old Sheriff. had with the Mayor. They were like f*ck buddies plus I don't thinking the Sheriff cares for me.

"Hey you…come on inside and sit down for a moment." Sheriff said.

The sight of him standing there while introducing me to several of his Deputies and his Secretary.

"This is going to be very brief." Sheriff said.

One of his deputies handed me a sworn statement.

"Mayor just write in your own words about your ware about and keep it simple f you can sir." Deputy said politely.

I had done exactly what he wanted, the sight of him returning back in the room they all left me in.

"Looks good Mayor and I like to thank you for your time for coming down and this statement, I'm sure that is going to be a big help to our investigation Mayor." Sheriff said.

"So, Sheriff, I hear you from Texas." I said

He stood there for a brief moment.

"I was born and raised, it the best place in the world with its wide open space and mountains with never ending stars." Sheriff said.

The sound of him laughing.

"You know it used to be nice and now it nothing but one big infested rats nest." Sheriff said. "Well, I wouldn't call it that but thousands upon thousands are now living breathing working doing what they can to improve the land Sheriff. I said.

"Maybe but my once open homes is now filled with big cities to small towns with and overcrowding growing population of peoples of all nationalities." 'Not to mention those that are escaping from America and Mexico. Sheriff said.

No matter how much criticism we took yearly, this country was ours to do as we please with.

"Sheriff, if I may ask...what do you think of the Whitfield case, seeing how you and the former mayor was working together on it?"

"Why you ask Mayor?" Sheriff said.

"Curiosity Sheriff." I said.

He stood there looking straight ahead.

"The young kid was in the wrong plus he put his hands on a man of the law and I feel that he's getting off easy only because of the money that his family has and even more so, the influence he has on this country."

"What would you have done Sheriff?" I ask.

"That's above me but you control that now Mayor." The sheriff said.

We stood there looking at each other for a brief moment.

"You know I haven't gotten of the Whitfield's incident." Sheriff said.

"I have no idea what you're talking about, is this something you had going on with the former mayor?" I ask.

It was true and now, it was up to me to give him what he wanted.

"So Mayor, now that you are in charge... What're you going to do with the Whitfield kid, you know you can just send him home if you wanted to." Sheriff said.

He was right and with that I had a lot to think about Mr. Pushing up Daisies was on the verge of releasing him, he knew his career wasn't going to go past the seat that I sit in now. But I have bigger plans and if I stand my ground with all that is going on and serve my time. I could run for governor and use that as a stepping stone to something much greater. Something tell me that the Board had a lot to do with Whitfield releasing but I had to be stronger and push it forward. There maybe even a profit to be made from this if I play my cards right and I had to stay several steps ahead of that old thyme noisy busy body Sheriff.

Chapter 19

County Corner Department

I had found my way back to the office an ended the day with a prayer among all the worker, everyone seem to be emotional over our tragedy still. It was understandable as the prayer was for his family strength but it was time to get back to work now. That following morning I had gotten another visit from that noisy old Sheriff. He was becoming a major pain in my ass.

"Good morning Sheriff, what brings you to my place of business?" ***I ask.***

"Well Mayor, it's like this as I was reading your statement…You claim that you were in your home and you must to have drank a little more than you intended to, well…I could understand that, I used to like the sauce once myself but now I'm an old man and my body isn't the way it used to be." 'You'll be like me one day and I see that you had a sip or two already."

"It's going to be a long day Sheriff and you're right, it helps me to relax." I said.

"Like I said Mayor, I was once a young man and enjoy the sauce myself back in a day but not anymore and did you know the former mayor wasn't even a drinker."

"I do Sheriff, he was a religious man but back in the day as you say, I knew him to enjoy the sauce himself…of course in his younger year's Sheriff and is there anything else I can do for you Sheriff?" I asked.

"You know Mayor, it's funny that you ask me that… remember how I was talking about those papers on the Whitfield kid that I needed and they had to be signed." 'You happen to have those right now signed?"

"Not at the moment Sheriff, I haven't had time to review them and all this is so new to me…you may have to give me a few days before I get them to you." 'And with you been so busy and all, there's no need for you to just…surprisingly show up" 'I'll have them delivered to you Sheriff."

"That's very nice of you Mayor, but as you know I'm used to come in here, especially unexpected…you see me in the former mayor was really good friends and I'm sure you are aware that." 'But now he's gone and I'll do my best to at least give you a call before making my way over here."

"That's very considerate of you Sheriff and I'll be looking forward to that call…before you come next time Sheriff." I said in a deeper authority tone of voice.

He just stood there looking down at me, even after I offered him a seat, this old man was becoming a problem that needed to be taken care of immediately is all I was thinking. It was a moment that he started to leave, but just as he got to the door and almost about to close it, he had stopped and looked back at me.

"Oh, by the way Mayor…I was wondering if you have the time would you like to come with me over to the Corners Office."

"Sheriff, I would really like to but I have so much work I have to do today, maybe next time." I said.

"Mayor, it's only going to take about an hour of your time and seeing how it is so early in the morning, this would be the perfect time and I'm just as busy as you are." 'But if we are to solve this case, I may need your help from time to time… seeing how we both have an interest in getting down to the bottom of this." 'Don't you feel the same Mayor?" Sheriff ask.

It was that moment, I had gotten on the phone and inform Charnel and Ms. Glasco that I was going to be out with the Sheriff for short time.

"Sheriff, I'll meet you over there." I said.

He just stood there looking at me while countering what I just said.

"Mayor, you can ride with me and I'll make sure you get back." Sheriff said.

This was going to be a very long ride with this old man but I could do nothing but accept the ride along with him. The silence was amazing between us, he didn't run his mouth as much as I thought he would as we arrived at the Coroner Department. This was one place that I was never fond of, it was like I could hear the voices of the dead. The second the door open, I felt this strange vibe of death, my hair felt like it was rising, this alone told me the spirits are with us.

I never like death but somehow I have always found my life around it, the Coroner had greeted us knowing he was expecting us. It was that moment that I had been introduce before we had taken the long stroll to my worst fear that awaited my arrival. I had known about this place for years but this was my first time actually been inside. The Coroner had took it upon himself to give us this the grand tour, we even walked inside a couple of rooms that was filled with nothing but death.

The sight corpse being cut up by his Staff Members to be examine was something I had no intentions on seeing today. But it was before my face and there was no way of avoiding it as we continue walking, the sight of him opening up this darken door. I could hear their voices, their screams fighting for their lives, the second the door opened, it caused me to freeze where I stood.

Their voices got louder noticing the Sheriff looking at me like if I could see the dead standing, as he glanced in the same direction I was looking.

"Are you okay Mayor?" He ask.

There was nothing I could say while feeling him somewhat shaken me.

"They don't bite, you two come on in here." Coroner said loudly.

I move slowly as a Sheriff kept pushing on my back to move faster while slightly laughing.

"You are a big boy Mayor."

There they laid as I counted five corpse on next to each other draped with a white sheet, each one had his own number alone with their own sound of death.

"What's wrong with you son?" Coroner ask.

"Nothing sir, it's just hard to imagine the death I see before me, it is sad sir."

"I know how you feel young man, I been doing this for so long and it never seems to amaze me, how life has no age when it comes to death son." Coroner said.

I watched him walk around the corpse, the sight of removing the white sheets, it was hard for me to look at them this way.

"Well, Sheriff, this is what burnt bodies look like, is not much because most of the evidence was destroyed." 'This is what is left Sheriff but we got a good team and we are doing our best, there is a Specialist about 200 miles away." 'I'm trying to get her here, maybe you can help." Coroner ask.

It was that moment, he had picked up some sort of utensil showing us exactly what they had been doing and we could see everything. Nothing about this was pretty, it was messy but I guess that comes with this type of job.

"Hey, Sheriff, here's something we found really amazing." Coroner said.

He had given us some type of cream and told us to rub it under our nose so we won't be able to smell what's about to be revealed. There was this one corpse, that hadn't been uncovered.

"You boys are about to be amazed at how cruel humans can be, this really is a shocker." Coroner said.

We watched him unzip this plastic bag, the smell alone was almost unbearable but the corpse itself wasn't burned like the others. It was still intact as if it had been sitting out in the burning sun baking.

"See how sick this bastard is and I hope both of you do your best to find this monster because he is still out there." Coroner said loudly.

I could tell this man had taken this to serious, his life revolved around death but somehow, this one had really gotten under his skin.

"Look you too, she was pregnant and even worse the child died inside the mom, maybe from suffocation and we found something else." Coroner said.

The sight of her walking toward the freezer as he called us over toward him, he had shown something that they had taken out the pregnant mom.

"Look, Sheriff you to Mayor, whomever this sick bastard was, sexually raped her, he was even stupid enough to leave semen inside of her." 'Sheriff all we need to find out is who this belong to and we

**got our killer or killers. 'I myself know it was more than just one."
Coroner stated.**

"How would you know that sir?" I ask.

They both just looked at me, like if I was a suspect or something.

**"Well Mayor, the DNA in this semen is a mixture of at least two
individuals, it may be more but we are working with what we got."
'These really are some sick mutha f*ckers!" Coroner yell.**

I listen to both of them talk but I have become speechless as he spoken
about the daughter as well, he stated the same thing about both twin girls
have been raped the same. We listen to him criticizing the bastards that
could do such a heinous crime as I said nothing about what he had been
talk about.

**"Hey Mayor, you look a little bit shaken up, this is not your line of
work…much different from office work I guess." Coroner said.**

*It was that moment, my eyes grew big…the sight of each of them raising up off the
bed and there was no sound from any of them until they touched the floor. The twin's girls
had begun to scream to the top of their voices while the mom looked at me holding her
stomach. The sound of her unborn baby could be heard crying, it was that moment. I saw
the twins get in front of their mom on their knees.*

*She stood there, her legs spreaded and before me the baby had come into this world
being held by his teenage twin sisters. I watched the mom take the baby and she cradled
it in her arms while the Mayor himself stared into the birth of his son. I found myself
backing away until the wall had stop me, the Mayor Philips himself has started to make
his way toward me holding his son. The moment I tried to move, his twin daughters he
blocked my path.*

*I could hear the Sheriff and the Coroner asking me if I was okay and what the hell
was going on with me. It was strange how they could not see any of this and yet Mayor
Phillips had walked between both of them as they stood looking my direction. His strong
voice echo throughout the room as I continue trying to escape but there was nowhere to go.
He held his son directly in front of me, the floor burn beneath him and I could see this
and his little baby burning before my face from that of a normal birth.*

That moment I felt the Mayor Phillips grab hold of me saying how my soul is wanted in hell and it was him that was going to take me there. I done what I could to get loose, I had hit him so hard that he went to the floor, it was that moment I felt the twins grab me. They had taking me to the floor as I done what I could to get away from these demons.

"Calm down Mayor." Sheriff said loudly

When it was all said and done, it was nothing more than several people holding me down, the sight of the corpse was still on the table. I had gotten up making my way toward the door and as I look back, there they all stood, standing by the corpse. The mother even had her crying looking at me, we ending up leaving and the Sheriff had personally giving me a ride back.

"Hey are you ok Mayor, you really freak me out back there." Sheriff said.

I had giving him some lame story about the fear I have of death, the Coroner had accept my apology for slugging him a good one. I had been told by the Coroner that he has been in this business for a long time and with his old age.

"Mayor I never seen such behavior like that in all my life and you acted like if I was been attacked by the family itself." Coroner said.

We had finally arrived back at my office and it wasn't a moment too soon. The second I was away from the insane Sheriff, asked me if he could interview some of my Staff concerning the former mayor.

"Sure, Sheriff, we will be more than happy to cooperate with you anyway possible." I said.

Chapter 20

Apparitions

I had taken several drinks the second I had arrived back in my office.

"Why have you been so isolated and what with this weird behavior lately." Charnel asked.

The rest of the day I kept looking around knowing what I saw with my own eyes, those corps had come to life before my face and no one else saw nothing. That crazy Sheriff definitely had e in his radar now from the way he lifted those thick silver scared eye brows and from the way I acted but it was those dam bodies coming to life. Charnel had come later on that day informing me of the Sheriff had come to interview them.

"Dam does that man ever rest!" I said loudly

I gather everyone together and told them to just be honest and cooperate because there statement may help out with the ongoing investigation. It was long after that I found myself back at home, it was a good time to look over documents that needed attention and signing. So much time had gone by that I was a maze when I looked from the balcony the moon was full.

"N*ggas will acting up tonight for sure." I said to myself.

My bed was like paradise the moment I found my way into it.

Sleep had come to me easily but I have been awaken by some strangeness that was taken place in my home. My eyes could barely focus as I looked over into the darken corner, I don't know how fast I had gotten up but I did. Whatever had appeared in that area had vanished the moment I flipped on the light, my heart pounded from what I just seen. The nine I now held my hand would have been useless, it was nothing more than a ghost appearing in the darkness.

It had been hard for me to go back to sleep, the light from my 250 gallon tank lithe made me feel a little more relaxed. There was this strangeness that remained as I left to work.

"Good morning." Ms. Glasco said.

There was no need to stand there and chat knowing this woman liked nothing about me, she would have chop my head off herself.

"Good morning." I replied back.

I stopped, there was no reason to be rude as I wished her the same knowing she was watching my every step.

"You've a morning meeting in about an hour from now." Ms. Glasco said before leaving.

Several quick shots gotten my morning started before Charnel came into my office.

"Why are your eyes blood shot red and why are you drinking so early?" Charnel ask with her hands on her hips.

Hell this was nothing compared to what I had on my way over here.

"Why are you looking at me like that?" Charnel ask.

I was hesitant on asking her this question but I had to get it off my mind.

"Charnel, you're into that spirit voodoo witch craft demon stuff right?" I asked.

"Why you ask if you already know the answer." She responded.

"Remember how I would be sleep and somehow when I woke up, you were there looking at me?" I said.

"Let me see, why I remember it different than that, every time I visited you, you was between some b*tches kitty cat...is what I remember. Charnel said.

"How did you transform your body like that into my house and somehow you would vanished into thin air." I asked. "It not voodoo or witch craft, you've to believe...see when the body dies, the spirit is still alive and free to travel into another form of life, now if you've a good soul...the creator who made it possible for you to come into this world give you the ability to returned but if you lived a bad life then his most precious angel who is now earth bound will also await your souls." 'But sometime the soul will get confused because it doesn't know that it has

passed or it may feel that it hasn't completed something while it was alive and remain earthbound." Charnel said.

She was starting to creep me out and I still didn't get the information I wanted.

"Okay, let's try this again, there has been some strange things going on in my house and last night I saw something that look like several individuals looking at me but when I turned on the lights, it vanished." I said

"How did it vanished?" Charnel ask.

"In the f*cking light or something, the shit wasn't there anymore but I felt like it was!" I yelled.

That moment she just sat there saying cum down before you sky rocketed your blood pressure.

"So, what you saw was spirits and if they are coming at you like that than it something they want from you and what've you done for spirits to be visiting you like that. Charnel ask.

I said nothing but the way she look at me had told her the story as she gotten up backing away from me.

"What is wrong with you Charnel?" I kept saying."

The way she kept looking around the room like if she was expecting something to happen.

"Mayor Phillips is here, his spirit hasn't moved on, maybe that why everyone has been experiencing crazy things happen to them, he must be trying to tell us something." Charnel had said.

"Okay, what do I do about these dame ghosts f*cking with me Charnel!" I ask loudly.

I watched her backing toward the door looking around, this was his office and everything I had was his, this was some nice shit and that n*gga want be needing it anymore. It was like my brother Jerry once said, one n*gga die another n*gga will come up and that just what I did.

"Charnel, what do I say to that n*gga when he show up again all ghostly spiritually like?" I ask.

The way she had looked at me had told the story that she didn't question me about it as I yelled at her again about what to say.

"You need to say, in the name of God…what does the dead want with the living until it goes away but it will become stronger with time,

as long as you breathe life, it will be drawn to you like the electricity that build up in us." 'We are all connected like gravity...the dead and the living." She shouted while leaving the room looking around.

I've never seen her afraid of nothing but somehow she has a weakness for bad evil spirits or something.

Chapter 21

Corps

I had a few more before the meeting of the Whitfield kid, Ms. Glasco had barge past Charnel only to inform me that the meeting was to take place but before she could leave. I had stopped her and asked if she could have a seat.

"Did you feel that?" Ms. Glasco ask.

I just looked at her, she was shivering while looking around as I kept saying in my mind what Charnel had told me.

"Ms. Glasco, you and the Former Mayor Phillips was very close to each other right?" I asked.

She just sat there.

"What are you trying to say?" Ms. Glasco ask.

"I meant work related and I'm going to need that same friendship from you and even more with this Whitfield kid, you know more about this case more than anyone and even with the formal mayor notes." "It hard for me to understand right now and I need you to explain more about this case, if you don't mind." "I would like to just put it to rest as easy and quietly as possible, if you understand what I'm saying." I said.

The look she had upon her face was none trust of me, I felt the hatred she had but we had to become a team as I tried to explained even more. Ms. Glasco had done exactly what I wanted, so much information and documents I never knew of.

"You see how Mr. Whitfield was to be return home but the final deportation paper was never signed and now you've that power" Ms. Glasco explained.

I had to take this in and figure out what to do as I was handed an ink pen.

"What is this for?" I ask.

"It's a pen Mayor, for you to sign." Ms. Glasco said politely.

I want to read them over to make sure everything is in order but she insisted that I go ahead and sign so she could get the papers to the next level.

"Ms. Glasco, that will be all, make sure everything is ready for the meeting and the donuts and coffee fund will no longer be compliments of the Mayor funding, if it is to continue." 'I would like you to work on some sort of share funding program involving the workers." I explained.

"How about the coffee and water, that is also funded by the Mayor, in which is now you." Ms. Glasco said.

"I never knew we had free coffee or water but now that you mention it, added that as well among the employees if it is to continue Ms. Glasco." I said.

She raised her nose up at me but I didn't care, the sight of that big wobbly ass was all she could give me. That would be my blessing if I could hit it before I terminate her uppity none loyal extra black ass. I had taken the information she had giving me and now I had to figure out what to do it after speaking to my Legal Advisor. It wasn't long after I found myself in another meeting, it was nothing more than another discussion over the Whitfield kid with the City Board Members.

"Mayor if I may address this issue of what is really going on with Whitfield Jr and are you really thinking of pushing this forward and you know that this has already been settle by the Former Mayor Phillips." Mr. Wyatt said.

"Mr. Wyatt, I'm aware but it was never signed before his death as you've been told right and you're right, I haven't officially been sworn in but my powers are just the same." I said loud and clear.

Several more voices had come into play, it was like they were talking in circles and over each other at the same time. I had said nothing until silence had come among their childish behavior.

"Thank you Mr. Robinson for explaining what they should've already known about Mr. Whitfield Jr. I said.

"I'm glad you recognized me, because you know that…shit rolls down hill and we're still at the bottom of a great Big Shit Hill and Mr. Whitfield Sr is holding that lid. I said.

"Mayor, he wants his son back home and safe without a scratch on him." 'All I'm saying is that this man imports so much to this country, his word alone is like that big bucket of shot waiting to be released upon us." Deputy Attorney Robinson said somewhat loudly.

It was amazing to hear so many different opinions about his released, so many kept telling me that it is the right thing to do. It was like if everyone was afraid of the outcome and how it was going to affect us in the worse way. I found this hard to believe but I wasn't backing down and I told all of them that I'm pushing the trail forward rather they supported it or not. Not one of them had giving me support, it was like if they thought we was going to be invaded with none stop bombing over one little rich bastard.

The problem I mostly had was with Deputy Attorney Robinson, he wanted an explanation for every decision I made over that kid as if it was his son or something. He wanted me to simply just sign the release form over to him and he would handle it from that point on. That commit alone had brought the meeting to an end as I had dismissed all of them after making the final commit. It was something that none of them wanted to hear.

I ended the meeting, not one of them approved of my decision as I gotten back to my office for a quick drink and Charnel had me about to burst through my pants but she whispered in my ear.

"Handle it yourself and someone wants to see you."

I had taking a moment to see who it was.

"Wow, hey kid…Justin right?" I said.

It was like looking at his dad but 200 plus pound lighter and 25 years younger.

"So you are the Mayor now huh, you know my dad said that you was smart enough to go all the way to the top seat if you really wanted it." Justin said.

"Justin, im so sorry about what happen to your family and if there is anything I could, please let me know and if it's financial." "Well, I don't have a lot but I can give you what I've" I said.

"Well, it's okay, because I know you loved him, remember how he use to take us fishing back in the day at Old Man Creek…remember?"

That was a long time when we were Boy Scout and camping with the rest of the neighborhood kids, his dad treated me like a son.

"I see that you're no longer little Justin, college life must be really good to you right now but I'm truly sorry about your family and I'm personally working with the Sheriff Department on getting down to the bottom of this." "We will find the ones that re responsible for this Justin, that's my promise to you and you still have my personal number right?" "I want you to feel free to call me anytime, you are my brothers. I told him.

The sight of him looking around had gotten me a little nervous.

"Hey, I was only a freshman when I help my dad sand off all that white paint and he restored all this old mahogany wood to its natural color." "It had taking me almost the entire summer to restore this place but it was worth and it was his ideal to put more windows in this room." Justin said.

"Your dad taught me a lot, he was an amazing man and we missed him very much around here Justine, so where are you living while you're? I ask.

"I'm staying at the house." Justin said.

I didn't know how to respond to him but I invited him into my home but he told me how he was ok.

"Hey would you like to have a seat." I ask.

We stood outside my office doorway like as he apologizing for not coming to see me earlier.

"Justin, we are doing all we can to find out he done to hideous crimes, I just want you to know that while you are here and if you hear anything that might help us." "I want you to come to me first and I will hold your hand all the way to the Sheriff Office my brother." I said.

Charnel stood listening the entire time, she heard every word before he left shaken her hand after I introduce them before he left.

"Sheriff is on his way to pick you up." **Chanel said with attitude. There wasn't much to say but wait, it wasn't long after I ended back at the Coroner Department.**

Coroner himself had kept his distance from me as he stayed by the Sheriff mostly, I told him how I was alright and it was a flashback.

"I have those from time to times from my Marine Corp." **Coroner said.**

I had to change the subject before he get into is war story that I couldn't match.

"Well you, there isn't much left to be done, we got hundreds of photo and DNA if we need it and these peoples need to be laid to rest by their families and love ones."

We all signed the closing investigation forms, I hesitated on getting to close to the corps thinking about what had happen before.

Chapter 22

The Funeral

That following morning was my relax time, it had been ruined after my first sip.

"Good morning Mayor." Said the old Sheriff.

He stood there grinning like if I was going to give him a large sum of money.

"Morning, what bring you here so early to my office without giving me time to prepare for your arrival but since you're here." 'Why don't **you come inside and have a drink even if it just one since you don't do the sauce anymore." I ask.**

"You have a great memory Mayor but I want to congratulate you on your swearing in as Mayor in few days I hear." Sheriff said.

"You hear very well Sheriff." I said.

"I'm sure you heard that the Mr. Phillips and his family funeral is going to be at the end of the week." Sheriff said.

"Yes, it is Sheriff as I spoken with his family seeing was there anything that we could do to help." I said.

"Well, was there?" Sheriff ask.

I told him ware it was to be held at his family church.

"So, Sheriff is there any other news regarding their family investigation or new from the Coroner Department." I ask.

"Nothing new Mayor but murder has away of surfacing without notice." Sheriff said.

"Do you have those papers yet" Sheriff ask.

"I'm still looking them over Sheriff."

My patient for this nosey grey hair old Sheriff was becoming less and less, maybe it was time for him to be joining Phillips and his family. This man as becoming a loose cannon. We talked a little more before the best sight I had was him walking away but as this day ended, another sunrise bought on a new one. It was amazing sight but being at Buffalo Soldier Cemetery had gave me a sense of fear.

So many visitors it saw daily, it alone was like work of art from it structure the United State Marine Honor Guards that made a special trip because of the Former Mayor history of once being one of them. They stood proudly full dress with everything shinning, everything thing upon them was well polished as I made my way through the crowed shaking hands and giving my deepest sympathy. Friends and family had come to give their least respect for what has been taking away from their lives. I had made my way toward Justin who sat with his family, he stood as I approached and the sight of so many had traveled so far just to be here.

"I can't take up much of your time Justine from your family but if there is anything I can do, I'm here for you." I said.

I took the time to shake each of their hands before leaving but it was that moment I could see the convoy of sadness entering the cemetery. Very awkward to look upon but it was what…what it was noticing everyone standing up the moment the pall burrier moved toward the Hurst's. They stood out like an army waiting for the drivers to stop, so many tears flowed the moment the rear doors had been open. It was like I could hear their voices the moment the coffin being pull out from each Hurst, it had become difficult to watch as they was now been carried.

There was even a pink baby casket that sat next to the mom that was no longer than a foot it had to have been the saddest sight. The concept alone that everyone had known that she was unborn and had to be taken from her momma and was now being carried by younger generation. Neither of them looked over twelve themselves, this was going to be a memory that they will have to live with for the rest.

We watched the Pastor stand over the caskets of the once a living speaking of theirs hopes and dreams, it was like speech after speech until the only living son of the family had spoken. So much none stop crying as I watch Justin stand up becoming the center of everyone attention. He spoke of his mom and dad and twin's sister and the one he would have meet when he came home for the summer this year. I had done my best of not hearing there screams of death that awful night as he continued to talk.

I wanted to leave but I stayed unknowing that I would be called up to speak as he announce me as his family. I had no choice but to say a few words of about the deceased, the sight of it all had become hard to look and the thought of the fire had left nothing but burnt blackness inside what look so appealing to the eyes outside. I spoke of the love we all shared and the loved they left behind and how this family were known to feed the homeless. I turned my head several times from the sight of Justin, it was like he face had become each of his family members. I could see the Sheriff noticing my odd movement alone with Charnel and Ms. Glasco, it was like if they were seeing me as the Devil in the flesh.

"It ok, you said enough." Justine said.

I had been escorted from the spotlight, that moment the Pastor joined in saying how I spoke from the heart. It was only a few more minutes later, the sight of them all being lowered into the ground slowly one at a time. The baby coffin was the saddest to see, she had been laid next to her mom, her cries could be heard from beneath. Gun blared into the sky form the Marines firing into the sky…Former Mayor Jacob Phillips had been honor and even I had been called once again to present his dad flag to him.

It was like a Hollywood scene but this was real, just like the tears that flowed none stop each. I found myself saying in the name of God…what does the dead want with the living every time something appeared that only I could see. I had even taking it upon myself to stay behind, even when everyone left as I stood over the fats ass Mayor bloated formaldehyde body.

"This was your fault Mayor, now look at you all f*ck up, you done this to yourself and in the process…it was you who killed your family fat ass, you thought a n*gga was soft and then you threaten to not just destroy me but an entire operation." 'Because you chose to be a b*tch ass snitch and for that." 'You had to get pop and now look at you the big political man, what do your wife and kids think of you now you fat overweight bastard and I hope that you burned in hell."

It was that moment I heard someone coming.

"Mayor, a few last word I see." Sheriff said

"Just a few Sheriff, saying my final goodbye to him and his family before I depart this cemetery Sheriff." I said.

"You know it's funny." Sheriff said.

"What is funny Sheriff?" I ask.

Oh, it's nothing, I was just thinking to myself about life itself." Sheriff said.

"You care to share Sheriff your wisdom of life." I ask.

"They say nothing ever dies, maybe the body does but the soul can something not give a man inner peace no matter how long he continue to live, now isn't that funny…a man can travel clear across the world in the most unknown area ever and yet he could still be hunted and hear voices of the dead." Isn't that remarkable Mayor?" Sheriff had said.

"I reckon say Sheriff." I said.

We had just looked at each other for a moment listening to the wind and birds alone with the silence between us.

"You know what is truly amazing Sheriff." I ask.

"I'm sure you're going to tell me Mayor." Sheriff said.

"Life is amazing Sheriff, look at this flower I'm holding, infect look at all of them…these flower are dead but they are so beautiful, even now in death and they grow from some of the worst elements known to man" I said

"What is the worst thing Mayor?" Sheriff ask.

"They grow from some form of manure of smelly shit and they blossom so pretty for the world to see, so many shapes and colors." 'They are like us, they want to stand out and they even reproduce just like us, the old dies and new ones are born to for the world like us Sheriff." 'Sheriff I don't hear voices nor do I believe in ghost or spirits and I hope you find out who committed these murders because there is a lunatic in my city and I personally don't like it Sheriff." 'You've a wonderful day and I don't want to be late for my swearing in today but you know that because you're a part of it right?" "This has been a sad day for all of us I said while tossing flower into each of their graves.

Chapter 23

Ghosts

That following morning, I had awaking to what sounded like screaming in my house causing me to hold Charnel tighter. She didn't hear a sound or even waken up when I tried to wake her. It was like as if it was meant for me and me only, whatever it was had definitely gotten my attention as I looked around the room. My heart beaten faster from fear alone but when she had awaken with this look I never seen before.

"Are you ok, look like you seen a ghost." Charnel said.

I could see her looking around the room very cautiously as I didn't have to say anything, she knew that we wasn't alone, she had this special spiritual ability to sense the unknown.

"You feel that huh." I ask.

She said nothing back but she had come from a long line of witchery and black magic.

"Yea there is a strange temperature change." Charnel said.

Our breath could be seen before our face.

"Something is here with us." I said.

My voice echo throughout this room while this crazy energy gotten stronger.

"Be strong and do not fear what hasn't allow you to see it for what it is." Charnel said.

She begun praying, it sounded like she was calling generations of her deceased for protection the moment she had gotten up from the bed. Her moving about the cold creepy darkness like if she was amongst whomever was in here with us without fear. I gotten up to turn on the light.

"Don't do that, I need to know why this spirit is here and why it hasn't found peace within its new life."

This was getting to freaky and crazy as I stood with my hand on the light switch, it was that moment that Chanel had taking notice my way even more."

"Don't move, you've a strong energy moving your way." Charnel said.

It was that moment I tried to turn on the light but my body had frozen solid like ice. It was like I was alive but I had no movement what so ever and I felt this buzzing energy of cold deadness had taking control of me entirely. I could see Charnel moving my way in the darkness but there was nothing she could do, her touch had no effect on me, it was as if I was nothing more than human brick wall. Something has appeared behind her, there was no face but its image over shadow both of us easily. Pick up from here

"You're not having a bad dream." Charnel said in the calmest way.

I sat there in silence looking at her look around the room before concentrating on me without an inch of movement.

"This spirit has un-finished business and vow to hunt you until death comes to you." Charnel said.

There wasn't much I could say but look at her sit there like if she was some sort of human statue or something.

"They will become stronger until it is able to inflict physical pain upon you." Charnel had said while holding my hand.

I was at a loss for words.

"What you've done to them in this world is over but they will remain earth bound making your life a living nightmare in their world of darkness." 'They want their daughter to be free and until that happen, they will not allow you inner peace.

"I've no idea what you're talking about Charnel

Charnel had just looked at me saying nothing more but her family will look over us tonight, she had told me to go back to sleep.

Chapter 24

The Girl

I sat there thinking and all that had come to mind was my cousin, it had taking me a while to find him after hitting several low life places that he was known to hang out. He was that true statement of how birds of a feather tend to flock together but I had several questions that needed to be ask. He was the man to see close and up personal, his eyes would tell me what I wanted to know even if nothing but lies come from his mouth. The sight of him been surrounded by nothing by rift raft and hoods and drunk women. It took me awhile but there he was.

"Hey, Mr. Bowen...may I have a word with you please as I interrupted his gambling game."

The sight of him standing up yelling at the others to watch his money before making his way toward me.

"Where is the girl Mr. Bowen?" I said.

"What girl cousin and why are you coming at me with this none sense at my place of business." 'You can't see that I'm on my lunch break?"

"Mr. Bowen, what we done can't be taking back and so many lives will never be above ground ever, it went wrong and nothing was right about that night."

"Like I said, I have no idea what you're talking about cousin and where are you getting this information from?" 'There is lots of girls around here if you go back inside and chose one I'll be more than happy to fork out the money for her but you can't be hogging it up because p*ssy become expensive after a while cousin."

I could do nothing but look at him knowing he knew what I was talking about, this was the time I wish I could put my 9mm right between that gold mouth of his.

"Mr. Bowen, what've you been eating because you've so much shit coming from your mouth and I need to know where that girl is like now." I ask once more.

"Cousin, where are you getting this from, did you see any others there that night accept for the ones we put to sleep." Mr. Bowen said loudly with aggression.

I stood there looking at him even more but I couldn't give into his ignorance, it's what he wanted.

"Mr. Bowen I know you've this young lady and you need to let her go and live what left of her life."

"First, I don't know what you are talking about and if I did, I would give you what you wanted but like I said cousin." 'Hey Ms. One Tooth, get that ass over hea!"

The sight of this scraggly looking hooker walking toward us looking like some sort of zombie or something with a cigarette in one hand and a brown bag in the other.

"Hey Ms. One Tooth, my man hea the mayor heard about your specialty that men's come from all around the world just to see you." 'He has come all the way from the Big House just to get a taste of what you're known for." 'I feel because he is a man of such great importance that you should give show him what you are known for on the house, see I'm looking out for you." 'You hook him up this one time, he goes back at tell his political boys and they all come down here and make that orange purse of your fatter with green backs." Mr. Bowen told her.

"You the mayor huh, I know it's you cause I saw you on that stoe TV over there days ago…you want this huh?" I had takin one look at her and told her how I wasn't looking for her specialty as I gave Ms. One Tooth a few dollars and told her to enjoy her day. I watched her walk away back to her corner counting what I has just giving her.

"That some flattering shit cousin, you made her feel like someone important, even more when you ask her, her real name." 'Personal you should have gotten a little what she is known for." Mr. Bowen said.

"I want to girl cousin." I said.

He stood there looking at me asking me if I ever just let shit go and how I need to mind my own business and stay out of his before saying what the f*ck while pacing back and forth.

"What do I get for giving the little b*tch?" Mr. Bowen ask.

"Lower your voice, we don't need to entire world knowing." I said. "So what do you want for her Mr. Bowen? I ask.

"A mil would be what I think she is worth." Mr. Bowen said.

"You crazy or what!" I said.

"Cousin, I know you been holding out on a n*gga all this time and that nothing but a dime to you and this ain't the time to be cheap when an innocent life is involve, especially one being blood related."

"Mr. Bowen, you don't I don't have that kind of money and this shouldn't be about money, it should be about human dignity."

"Bullshit cousin, you got your hand in everything including the city police and half the shit I don't' even know about." Mr. Bowen said.

"Mr. Bowen, this girl need to be free and I'll make it even with you eventually but you can't keep her, she is nothing more than a bad link." "Not to mention death by hanging in this country if we are lucky."

"Ok, later." Mr. Bowen said.

"No, I want to see her now Mr. Bowen."

He stood there looking at me while glancing at the crap game.

"Hey what yawl broke niggas doing over there and my money better be still be there he shouted loud enough for the entire world to hear."

*"That n*gga Broke Down just hit and got that money!" Someone shouted even louder.*

"See cousin what you just cost me and now you ole me bills cousin!" Mr. Bowen Shouted loudly with anger.

"Now Mr. Bowen." I said.

It was that moment he made his way back to the crap game before we had left, my cousin had this strange way of doing thing. He always preferred to take his own car but then again, it was safer for me as it was no telling what he just done or who was out looking for revenge when it came to him. I had followed him, we past few spots where I thought he had her hidden but he kept driving, he had asked me to turn off my cell phone. It was understandable because we've done this nemourios times before, therefore I had no way of contacting him.

The area he was going to could be nothing no more than a mistake or make he took a wrong turn. I know this n*gga can't be this f*cking stupid to be using this area especially after what recently just happen here involving our own Federal Police. We finally arrived and all I could say is that he is this stupid and I would have to seen this to believe it. The moment I stood before him, the only thing I could ask was that I know you can't be this stupid as he just looked at me.

"Welcome to Crawford Mill cousin." Mr. Bowen said.

He stood there and all I wanted to do was knock him the f*ck out where he stood but there was another issue to be taking care of right now.

"Follow me cousin." Mr. Bowen said loudly.

The sight of 3 of his boys was inside standing about and judging from the scattered cigarettes butts and alcohol and fast food wrappers scatter. They had been here for a while noticing the little generator with gas jugs scatter about, they had been set up for living but why is all I wondered. We made our way through the long creepy hallways and up three flights of metal stairs before we had come to where they held her. The way he laugh while removing the master lock from the door.

"Cousin don't get your panties in a bunch."

"Meaning?" I ask.

"Sometimes you have to do what you have to and she may not be a pageant contestant right now but she is in the break down process but she is to strong minded."

"Yao know, they filled her way of thinking with love and all." Mr. Bowen explained.

The moment he open the door. There was the most horrible smell ever hitting me like a storm, my nose needed replacing. The room along was unfit for your enemy to live, not even fit for wild animals.

"Help me." It was all I heard from her weaken voice.

The room was scatted with used condoms it told me that she had been rapped daily and beaten as well, her face was badly bruised and her legs looked like they had been pulled apart from the many bruises. I could only imagine the way she was been held down.

"Here she is cousin, all in one piece and if I may say from experience…she has something wonderful down there that worth big money for years to come. Mr. Bowen stated.

"What the f*ck have you done to her?" I said.

"Like, I told you cousin, she was really tough to break but we almost got her broken…few more days and she will drop panties upon demand."

"How long have you been drugging her?" I ask.

"Cousin we giving her the normal but I had to double the dosage from time to time, she is almost hook on the shit now." Mr. Bowen said.

"What is your plans for this young lady and how did you get her, she wasn't in the house that night." I ask

He stood there saying nothing until I ask him again.

"Well cousin, you left a little early as always that night, I stayed behind to make sure the fire destroy everything." 'But the moment we were about to leave the house, she enter screaming to the top of her voice, maybe it was the way her parents was tied up and gage." 'But they were already forever sleeping, my boy No Neck wanted to sing her a lullaby but when I saw her pretty, she was I saw nothing but money." Mr. Bowen explained.

"So you brought her hear of all places, do you remember what just recently happen here?" 'And why would you think this place is still not under watchful eyes Mr. Bowen.

"Cousin you worry too much about nothing and what happen is in the past now wouldn't you say and why would they want to return here?" 'Wouldn't you think they moved on to bigger and better?" Mr. Bowen said.

"No, I don't and what're your plan for her?" I ask.

*"Well, she is yours for an easy mil or she end up on her back side or ass in the air or a cock been shoved down her throat, all for the right price." 'She is almost hook and learning to shut her mouth, I see big dollar coming my way for the fountain of youth, that she is and she just turned 18 several days ago." 'Prime grade p*ssy at its best cousin." Mr. Bowen Said.*

"You can't keep her, you can't transport her and you can't trade her for nothing." 'Mr. Bowen, this is the missing link that could link us to her family deaths, are you understanding that…she can't even be seen by anyone." 'I'm leery of those fools you've walking around here already, you know loose lips sink ships." I stated.

"You know what your problem is cousin, you don't trust anyone and you've faith in nothing but your own life and you need to relax and enjoy life a little now." 'You're the Mayor of this City now and all you need to do is relax and get all the in-office p*ssy you can while you have the power." 'You're a king now…you can't be a gangster anymore… remember what you've become and who gotten you that big seat." Mr. Bowen said

"You can't keep her." I said standing before him.

"Ok, than you tell me about what I should do with her Mayor?" Mr. Bowen said loudly. I stood there looking at him as he stood before me like if he was more puzzled than a n*gga who just got caught sleeping with the plantation Massa wife.

"I'm not sure, she has seen your face and once she describe you and she will the second she get free enough to run to the police." I said.

"Why do you care, how many girls have you destroyed with drugs dope and let not forget torture and rape…I recall cousin." Mr. Bowen said.

I could do nothing but walk around looking at him talking to myself until I was unaware that she was now looking directly at me.

"Now she see you cousin, we are all link to her now, what you're going to do now Mayor of the City of Liberation."

The way she look at me while my cousin held her blind fold in his hand looking at me himself as he kissed her on her filthy cheek. The way he expose her now hairy bush by pulling down her panties, the pinkness of her body could be seen when he pulled her lips apart.

"Don't that look yummy cousin, come on over here and hit it just like this, my hands along is on fire just from her touch…this young p*ussy is hot cuz." 'You can pound none stop until you bust, trust me… she can take it and more since she now knows who you're Mayor." Mr. Bowen said.

I watched her fight him the best she could but her hand had been tied and that filthy mattress and he had her chained to like a slave to old rusty metal bed.

"Come and get some cousin." Mr. Bowen kept saying while fingering her.

"You really are an idiot Mr. Bowen." I said.

It was that moment he pushed her back into the bed angrily, the sight of him rushing toward me like some mad man getting in my face.

"I'm the idiot cousin, Mr. Big Dog Uppity Mayor, it was me who took the blame for you, it was me who done your time!" 'It was me who gave up my young years so you can become the man that you are now!" 'That was all me and I'm the idiot cousin!" 'You made me this way and in this country, if you're a convict...then you're nothing from that day forward!" 'I'm what you made me Mr. Mayor...you made my life worthless."

I stood there looking at him knowing it was best that I said nothing back right now as I needed this fool to just calm down...before I smoke his ass. His loudness had brought his crew this way as they now all stood by the door saying nothing. He was always a magnet for low life just like himself.

"Hey you need to calm down, there is no point in you acting like a fool...not that anyone would hear you anyway." I said.

"Listen to me Mr. Uppity, since I'm such an idiot, this is what I come up with in my head, we took around 315.000 dollars from the Mayor house, all open cash...we got broken off a little but you are holding the majority of it." 'I'll drop the mill if you give me the reminder and we call it even cousin." The fool said.

I could do nothing but look around the room as I step to him politely and asked if I could have a few words with him. He had only giving his fools enough money to survive on, two of three of these fools now drove better cars that was park outside. They called themselves been hidden but yet old school luxury cars could been seen in broad day light.

"Cousin, look at those clowns, are you sure you can trust them, I going to tell you why I decided to keep the money until things die off for a while." 'You gave them G's huh?' 'Have you notice what they are driving, there bringing too much attention to not just themselves but you as well." 'Don't you think they would knock you off themselves if they knew you had it, they're not loyal to you Mr. Bowen and if there

was a reward out right now, do you think they would turn you in?"
I ask.

He had done nothing but look at them none stop and he had notice them wearing expensive shoes and gold chains. I hope I was getting in that big stupid head of his…hoping some light comes on.

"I trust them cousin, it's you that gives me a nasty feeling inside lately and if you want that girl, it's going to cost you." 'You know what I want so…make it happen cousin because I'm winning either way." Mr. Bowen said roughly.

"Listen, Mr. Bowen, we could go all the way to the top" I said

"You want to be Governor?" Mr. Bowen ask.

He was such a dumbass, maybe even from birth.

"No, I want the bigger but that would be the right step but we have to be smart and play the game." I said.

"So, im supposed to be walking in your shadow all my life or do I have to remind you that I'm convicted felon and I can't have a life in politics." 'So do I hold the key to your success is what I'm hearing and it's like I said so start paying me my duckets." 'We been talking enough cousin." Mr. Bowen said loudly.

We stood there looking at each other.

"Look at his fountain of youth cousin, do you know if I fry her brain to nothing." 'I want have to worry about her attitude never again and she would be nothing but a hole to f*ck." Mr. Bowen said.

He was crazier enough to make her that way.

"You know that's at least 10 years of good nut busting ass f*cking deep throating and I could breed her for babies and maybe make even more top dollas." 'That what I have here cousin…this is my big seat."

"Mr. Bowen we can't keep her. I said.

"Have you ever had chocolate Mexican taco salsa cousin?" Mr. Bowen said.

I said nothing.

"You take a good prime piece of p*ssy like her and you pour salsa right between the crack of her goodness…mild of course and you just enjoy your chocolate taco."

"You really are a sick disturb mentally challenge bastard aren't you." I said.

He said nothing while looking my way licking his finger after smelling it.

"Now that some good smelling sweat tasting fountain of youth and you sure you don't want some of this cousin?" Mr. Bowen said.

"Mr. Bowen, you have to let her go and maybe that not even the correct answer but we have to do something with her." I said.

"You can kill that noise rush me the money cousin." Mr. Bowen said.

"I need you to be smart and not stupid or an ignorant n*gga that you are being now." I said.

"I'm ignorant cousin, you just got life all twisted in your political world but if you don't got my money than you need to be leaving." Mr. Bowen said.

It was that moment he moved toward her like a mad man reaching at her insanely while she tried to resist him. She screamed loudly when he begin tearing off her panties while ripping them from her body, the more she fought the more he beat her.

"Shut the f*ck up b*tch!" Repeatedly he yelled.

He penetrate her body talking shit the entire, the way he treated her only told me that she couldn't live past this room. She had too much anger from all that has happen to her and her will power was too strong for her to just forget and walk away. It was that moment I moved toward both of them but had been stopped by his boys at gun point, I could do nothing but put my hand up and watch. I had known these fools for a while but they were loyal to my cousin and definitely not me.

"I'm leaving." I yelled.

I'm surprise they just let me walk away but they made a mistake and that was not taking my gun as I could see them from the outside small window. They had been gang rapping her from the way both of them was getting ready to go next. Without hesitation I storm back into the room and put one right in the back of Sammy Tee neck but that didn't kill him. He tied to return fire but I put two more shots in his face, he feel into me somehow as I caught him. Ruckus blasted with the sawed off ripping Sammy Tee entire gut from his body killing him instantly.

I heard him trying to rack on more into the sawed off when I fired again killing him dead but put one more in his head just to make sure. It was that moment my cousin was already trying to reach for his gun while still inside her.

"Are you f*cking crazy! M. Bowen yelled.

"Yes…you made me this way."

That I realized the best medicine I could give her was death, it was that moment I looked at her.

"May you joined your family in heaven."

I put one in her head while he jumped from her body talking shit but I knew I counted four of his thugs and they would be on their way. My cousin aggressively charge my way as I caught him across the head with my 9 mil knocking him to the floor. I heard them coming down the hallway fast as I pulled the sawed off from Ruckus hands and gotten behind the door. I gotten both of them when they rushed inside one by one killing them dead. It took me a second to get to my feet's now standing over my cousin looking down on him.

"Don't kill me he shouted." "I should but this was never about killing you Mr. Bowens, we are family and I tried to work with you on this one and now look at the bloody mess we caused." I said softly like.

"What now!" Mr. Bowen yelled.

"You have a messed to clean up." I said.

It was that moment he gotten up looking at me after really looking around angrily.

"You are f*cking crazy cousin and this shit ain't over!" 'It's over and you have to job to finished, this was your fault and no one else's." I said.

I wipe the sawed off down and gave it to him and walked away until I heard him rack one in the chamber, my heart beated.

"Mr. Bowen, the only way im not leaving this room is…you are going to have to out one in my back." I said.

It's was that moment, I heard him blast one into the ceiling.

"You shot her while I was in the p*ssy…you are f*cking crazy and this shit is not over cousin!"

I didn't even look back before quietly walking away saying nothing.

Chapter 25

Old Man Johnson

I arrived at work after a long harsh unforgettable weekend and all I could hope was that Development had forward the information I requested and that Charnel had it on my desk. The moment my car had arrived, it was time for breakfast, my driver was a little different than the others. He was a wise guy, convicted felon known and Bones, he knew the street as well as everyone that operated in them. I recruited him from through this hoodrat that I used to mess around with on the side.

She is long gone but he is still here, it wasn't never my plan to have him become my coffee boy, this was something he done on his own. I always thanked him each time for such dedication at its best or the places I often found myself in at times. You need someone like him because he was the street as I'm sure he still does his share of dirt, it the way street niggas like him operate. It simple, he does what I want and I do my best to stay out of his business and he does mine the same. We have and understanding of each other, this shit was more than good as I enjoyed every bite.

That morning I had coffee listen to one of the employee make un-call for commit, I ignored it as I finished my breakfast burritos in my office. Charnel enter my office with the information I wanted and she told me that nothing was schedule accept for the normal meeting and Mr. Johnson had called in saying he could come in after lunch along with several others behind him.

"Mum no drinking this morning Mr. Pope?" Charnel ask.

I said nothing as I lifted up my coffee cup, plus this stuff help to wake me up in the morning when alcohol kept me mellow throughout the day. This stuff was highly needed with this new position and meeting throughout the day plus it wasn't that bad once you get used to it.

"Good job Mayor, not to mention how you're giving your kidneys a break for once." Charnel said.

"Is there anything that you could be doing other than been in here messing with me?" I asked

"I leaving Mayor and thanks for coming to see your son, he really enjoyed your time, you made his day better and now I hope you can continued making time for your son." 'You know if we were married, you could see him daily." Charnel said while smiling.

I watched her leave, knowing that thang was making her feel all womanly inside as she smiled leaving the room. This was the beginning of my day but with all that was going on I had a chance to come back inside and have a rum and cola with crushed ice and cherries, it all come together so well. The moment Charnel had come over the sound power telling me that Mr. Johnson is waiting to speak with me. I thanked her and told her to send him inside.

"Good morning Mr. Jim Johnson Jr." I said.

He stood there looking at me like if he ole me money or something while looking around the room, if your appearance said a million words about you. I would say this was a hardworking man who seem to be struggling with life daily from the way he dress. You would think a man who owned so much would be looking like nothing but money, but obvious he represent a different type of land owner.

"Have a seat Mr. Johnson, make yourself comfortable." I said.

It was that moment I asked Charnel to come into my office.

"Hey, I want a cup of coffee and something sweet." I ask.

She stood there looking at me like what the hell.

"Mr. Johnson would you like something?" I ask.

She caught on to the entire dog and pony show.

"I'm be ok Mayor." He said.

But I insisted that she bring him the same as I having. It had taking her a few minutes but from the time she left until the second she returned, his eyes was glued to her jiggling ass the entire time. Shit, I don't blame him as I enjoyed it every chance I could get. I just smiled when he notice me looking at him as he didn't even try to play it off as he bitten into the donut she had giving him and drank his coffee. It was that moment.

"I want to apologize for not taking the time to shake your hand Mr. Johnson." I said.

It alone told me of his awareness of everything around him, he seem so alive in an old school way wondering if he grew up in the world without contracts or signatures and lawyers. He was probably the time zone when your word and a handshake was all you needed of course that time zone is long gone sadly to say. He sat back down sipping on his coffee after adding a few more cubes of sugar.

"Mr. Johnson, is really good that you took the time out of your schedule to come on down here and visit me, even more so on the little information you got just to come down here." 'But something tells me, that you're going to be real satisfy when you leave my office, now I understand that your hard-working man and you come from a family of nothing but hard-working men's." 'Now I'm all right about that or I'm just blowing hot air at you Mr. Johnson." I said.

"Oh, you be right about those words and I be a hard-working man, no one is ever gave me nothing or my family from what I be knowing." Mr. John said.

I thought there looking at this man, he had a different type of vocabulary and I wonder if I sustained why am or become what he knows. Maybe it was just better, that I remain who he is already met and not try and change of my style, to cater to him.

"Like I said Mr. Johnson, I'm glad to see you on such short notice."

"Okay there Mayor." Mr. Johnson said.

Silence had become a part of us as we stared at each other for a brief moment.

"Mayor, what you be wanting widow me, did I do some wrong or does law had trouble with me." Old Mr. Johnson said somewhat loudly.

"Mr. Johnson, are you a TV man and do you watched the news." I ask.

"Yeah I do, I be watching my westerns and like that movie they call cops...you know I saw some of my young relatives on the show, they be out there doing all kinds of wrong thangs but they don't be listening to

old me, they be calling me confused an old tyme but that's okay." 'The
youngin don't be knowing nothing about nothing, they just be ignorant
all these days of a life... just plain stupid is what I be seeing in a lazy
generation" 'you know Mayor they don't even want to work these days.
Mr. Johnson said.

I just looked at this man, if I cut them off from asking a few questions
more, he will do just talking about nothing but some lazy ass boys in his
bloodline.

"Mayor, what does the TV got to do with old man Johnson is all I
want to be knowing right now."

"Good question Mr. Johnson, I see your man of wisdom and intellect and
you give a strong presence will not tell you why you hear Mr. Johnson and I
love the way that you're being straightforward." 'You remind me of myself
when I started playing this political game and I wanted nothing but straight
answers from real people just like yourself Mr. Johnson and that's why I ask
you to come down here and sit with me while we discussed his business that
you may like." I said.

"Mayor I got a lot of work that needs to be done today and I don't
have a whole lot of money, so I do it myself and if you can see." 'I'm not
young like I used to be." Mr. Johnson said.

He just sat there, sipping on his coffee while eating doughnuts knowing
he shouldn't have been eating that many. But I like sugar, it tends to give
people more energy and it makes them faster to react instead of sitting back
observing everything, yes…sugar is amazing no matter what form or how
it travels into your body.

"Mr. Johnson, now you are the owner of Freedom Park right and
before we get really started I just want to give you some information
on that piece of land." 'With such a large amount of land in the profits
that you intake yearly, you are barely make enough to pay your own
property tax right?" 'Now, I could be wrong but I'm looking at your
past payment history and I see that you have several missed payments."
'It alone has made you pay extra and penalties, now…am I correct Mr.
Johnson?" I ask.

He just looked at me saying nothing but when I gave him the
documents, his facial expression told me all I needed to know. He remove

some dingy looking eyeglasses that was so scratch…they should have been scrapped as his gray looking eyes concentrate deeply on reading.

"Mayor, I know I be having trouble at times but even with a costing me more money, I always be paying my taxes and I never have to deal with them that much." 'So, tell me what all this be about Mayor?"

"Mr. Johnson, we have a problem." I said.

It was that moment that I had gotten up, it was easier than I thought as I found it on some station that would explain the reason why he was here. It only taken me a second for him to figure it out. I stood there looking at him.

"See, Mr. Johnson, that why you're here and since you own Freedom Park and I'm sure that you are aware of the Whitfield kid." 'The punishment that he is about the face, is nothing new but there is something that hasn't been done before." 'Mr. Johnson, has any of those boys in and your family or you face public punishment." I said.

"Yeah, my little nephew James Jr, well…he had been given five lashes for assaulting a police officer while resisting arrest and after he served three months, part of his jail time had been suspended because he chose public lashings.

I didn't want to get into a long conversation with this man as I ended up shutting him up about what I had asked.

"So, Mr. Johnson as I see that you are aware of what is going on in the city concerning the Whitfield kid and with this said Mr. Johnson." 'The official site that this type of punishment normally takes place is not big enough for what I want to happen." 'Your park is more than big enough for this public event of Mr. Whitfield Jr punish for the crimes he committed." I said.

"I don't quite understand what you talking about Mayor and why you want my property, all that trash will be left behind, people doing damage and it will be me who cleans it up…when everybody's gone." 'I'm a going to have to say no Mayor, is just too much work for me to do afterwards and you see I'm an old man." 'It's becoming harder for me to move around these days.

I sat there looking at this man knowing he is probably right but with the money he could make, the cleanup wouldn't even scratch the surface of the money he would make.

"Mr. Johnson, I want you to take the time to look at these numbers, especially the amount of money you will be able to make if you allow me to use your park for this public punishment." 'I have taken a time to highlight certain areas especially the last page." 'Mr. Johnson there should be at least 50,000 peoples now here is how it's going to work, you charge those number you see written and half for kids." 'All I ask of you is 20% of the profit.

"Is there a contract." Old man Johnson ask.

"No contract a handshake and trust between us will do." I said.

"Mr. Johnson do you like those numbers at the bottom of that page...that's what you are expected to make."

"Lot of money here." Old man Johnson said.

"This is going to be a one day affair and nothing more, there is no tomorrow or the day after and those numbers that you see, should happen on that day."

"That be a lot." Old man Johnson said.

"Now Mr. Johnson from my calculation, you would have to be a young man and work to the age you are now to even get close to numbers like those... wouldn't you." 'I'm a man of my word Mr. Johnson and if you knew the former Mayor, he was also a man of his words and I learned from him before he left his world. I said.

"It was him that I voted for." Mr. Johnson said.

I listen to him a bit more talking about nothing that was important to me.

"This is your prayer answered, now how about it Mr. Johnson, are you willing to play ball and retire like a rich man from one day of work." I would if I was you and you know there is nothing to think about." I said.

"Well, what about toilets and my ponds smells." Old man Johnson said. "I'll take care of that as well as the toilets, now are you willing to plat ball." I ask.

"How can you do on this Mayor and how can you make this happen with only days away for Mr. Whitfield punishment?"

"Mr. Johnson, it all starts which you and your park and from that point on, you have nothing to worry about and I could personally bring in attendants to help you with." 'There is nothing for you to worry about Mr. Johnson but

collecting money you don't have when it's all said and done and I'm working with the Governor to bring in our National Guard and I'll have the Police Department there alone with County Sheriff Department."

He stood there looking but I didn't have the time to play with his old ass.

"Mr. Johnson, I need a d answer now." I said.

It was that moment he grabbed his hat and d gotten up.

"Mr. Johnson wait!" Listen here, I tried to be nice to you old man, there is no time...now we can make money together or I write up a document for the need of the city and take your park today and your old black grey ass will not get one shiny penny." I said hostilely.

I watched him sit back down.

"I thought that might get your attention old man or was it the part that I may just take it all together with time." I ask.

He just sat there somewhat shaking realizing that I could take his entire life with my ink pen.

"No are you willing to play ball?" I ask.

"Yea, whatever you say Mayor. Mr. Johnson said sadly.

It was that moment we stood.

"Hey, its good politics to shake hands after a deal Mr. Johnson don't you think?" I ask.

He just stood there.

"Shake my hand old man, that an order from your Mayor...you can't win here." I said.

It was that moment as I held his hand tightly informing him that he was going to be working what a man named Mr. Bowen's.

"The gangster, that man's be a heartless killa of the worst kind and I don't know about working with him." "They be saying bad stuff about him!" Old man Johnson said loudly.

"Mr. Johnson, you have to trust me, this one is a one-time deal and I'll personally take care you, now Mr. Bowen's is a businessman and if you really know him." "You should know that he has many business under his belt like hotels...food establishments...sanitation department." I said.

"What about that cemetery, I heard he got part of that and that man is like sleeping with snakes with a full bellies...still don't mean they won't bite you." Old man Johnson said.

"Work with, it's only for a short while.

It taken a moment, there was nothing but silence between us as I let his hand go watching him stand saying nothing.

"You can leave now Mr. Johnson." I said several time before he finally left.

No smile what so ever but one thing we both agreed on that my cousin was a hurricane destroying everything in his path running around like a dog wildly. Shit his own boss was afraid of him and there was nothing I could do because he was known to put the fear peoples. I had to take a breather noticing more contractors waiting to see me.

Chapter 26

Freedom Park

That morning as I had gotten up, it was like clockwork somehow, my driver was at the door as he glanced inside when I open it up.

"Mayor, I had come a little early than normal, where do I drop this one off?" Bone ask.

The sight of him driving away knowing he would be back shortly, I only hope that he bring another one of those delicious burritos and coffee this time would be great.

The moment I had gotten back inside had giving me this funny feeling of coldness as I walk toward the thermostat. Maybe that hoodrat was messing around with it but it was on the normal temperature as I reach for my nemourios scattered bibles. There is no telling when you was going to need the Lord around here lately.

The sight of the folder seem like it was moving slowly when I was walking toward it causing me to freeze dead in my tracks again. I found myself breathing harder from fear before calling for that hoodrat only to realize that she just left. It hard to understand why I feared being alone, Charnel told me how she would move in but that wasn't the answer…plus it would only give her fuel to regulate my life. No women will ever get that opportunity, smelling the same p*ssy for the rest of my life on this planet, that worser than life in prison.

We were rulers in our own land but here we became slaves, ripping out heritage apart for ever but now we are becoming what we once were. The God of the universe didn't give *us all this long strong d*ck to be with just one woman. It belong to whoever, nemourios wives but Charnel believes in the old ways of America, she will never be broken from it. There was much for me to do but avoid looking at it until I heard it fall to the floor as I gotten away from it holding the bible.*

"In the name of God, what does the dead want with the living?" I kept saying repeatedly.

I found myself rushing to do what needed to be done before getting out of this creepy house, the sight of my driver pulling up was nothing more than a relief to see as I gotten in the car.

"It all that hot enough for you Mayor?" Bone had ask.

It was amazing, every bite couldn't be describe as the coffee was just the way I like it, I had to thank him once more. We had a bit of a drive, so it was time to just relax a little before getting to work but as I gotten there, the sight of the media was not what I wanted to see.

"Should' I find another area to park Mayor?" Bones ask.

I had taking a second looking around and just said no knowing they would find me somewhere else plus I had to deal with them today anyway. My first step out the door was nothing but cameras in all direction, my driver had gotten a few of them out the way as I made my way inside. There was nothing else I could tell them but, the law had been broken and how I'm sad that it had to come to this. The entire office had focus on me as well, Charnel had made her way into my office, she had a lot on her mind, my entire day was filled she stated.

The most important was a meeting of Mr. Whitfield involving the Governor himself who wanted to speak with me behind close door. The morning had begun to go into the noon hours and with all that has taking place, no one was leaving with a smile on their face but what did I care about what they thought. So much money is riding on this decision and there was no way I was going to call it off regardless of what them politician wanted. It had become time to get the show on the road, my driver had arrived, the sight of him at my door. I had invited him inside.

"Mayor, would you like a rum and coke." Bone ask.

I made a few more phone calls before leaving the building to see my police escort waiting due to all the threats that I have been getting.

"Mayor, we will be taking the back street into Freedom Park until we come upon the main entrance, there should be lots of protestors but you'll be under protection all the way to your seating." Officer Hartfield explained.

It was that moment I had gotten in my car, a small tour of the city before we had arrived, it was just as I had been told. This entire area was line with cars from people paying to get inside to the protestors scattered out the area getting louder by the second. Our white citizens young and old was aware of or rules and regulation but Mr. Whitfield had them fired up over racisms that I believe that not one of them was thinking for themselves. I thought this was going to be overwhelming but the media along has blown this completely above of what I expected.

There had to be every broad casting station known to man and they were all hear to cover the Whitfield kid about to get his ass beat like if he was Jesus back in the day. The sight of our military had been activated to not just help but it was going to be them that control this unruly crowed. Once they found out that I had arrived, it wasn't good as my vehicle had been vandalized by everything these idiots had in their hand. It had taking several minutes before the police to get this under control, I actually thought my car was going to be flipped as I sat there.

I felt sorry for them when the Army had been call to clear the area, they were ruthless as I watch them snatch peoples like if they were nothing. I watch one of them get hit so hard that he must to have busted his head, the blood he had left on my window. It was hard to believe that he still manage to get back to his feet before he had been taking back to the ground and arrested. It was long after that, a line had been formed on both side before I had gotten out of the car.

The second my door had been open brought nothing but kayos and madness, my first step outside of the car was noisy from people shouting curse words while other praise me for whatever reason.

"Mayor we are moving." Some Officer said.

The sight of the crowed would not let up none stop as I made my way to my seating area, I wave at the crowed but some of their responses wasn't what I wanted to hear as I kept waving while smiling.

"Mayor, I'm leaving several of my Officers near for your own personal protection."

I watched them leave while taking notice how many was actually here, I invested in three rat infested hotels and everyone is filled. The city alone was so full, it was like if everyone was making a profit from this little rich bastard. We need to do this even more to build the city economy.

"How are you Mayor?" Judge said.

The sight of her wasn't far from me, it had only taking few words of encouragement to get her to sit next to me. I watched her exchange seats, this was going to be very interesting as we could see cameras going off none stop. If she was only in the spot light for a brief moment before, that was now up for change. I watched her shy away from the photos taking of her but I told her what she already had known.

"It's better that you look your best than to have some crazily looking photo ending up front page new judge, trust me I know." I said.

I had begun laughing alone with my little entourage but she didn't find it funny as she looked at her husband who had joined us.

"Judge are you enjoying another busy day of work?" I ask.

I listen to her reply, she told me how she has never found this amusing but, I could do nothing but look her way especially when she said if she sentence someone. It would be hypocritical of her not to look of, there wasn't must to say. That commit was too overwhelming for me to even think of responding too, maybe she gotten a high from sentencing me in some lunatic freaky way or something.

"Ms. Antoin, you ain't no joke are you?" I said laughing like.

"This is never a joking matter or nothing to laugh at, don't you think?" Judge ask.

I guest so Judge." I responded.

"So, Judge. I see you don't travel with protection?" I stated.

"I being doing this for a long time and I never had the need for security but I see you travel with a lot and how long you expect to keep them around Mayor?" judge ask.

I had done nothing but look at her, there wasn't much to say and maybe I was nothing more than a little boy inside playing politics. The thought of her saying that had taking me back in to when I was the Vice Mayor, when the Mayor told me to get out of this career field because I wasn't a giver but a leech…searching for pray.

"So, Judge what is the outcome going to be since you seem to know so much from your years of experience, you think he will leave quietly back to the U.S.?"

"No, you know me and the former mayor had work this out, he ask me that same question and by now. Mr. Whitfield Jr would've been home doing whatever that he does." 'You cans still stop this before the first slash is giving…leaving him with a laceration that will leave a life time score alone with a burden of lifetimes pain and somehow you gotten the media involve." 'Personal…Mayor, I told you that this was a bad ideal."

"Judge, I can't take all the blame, it was you and him who made this happen…you even more because you sentence him if I'm not mistaking." 'You were brought here from Louisiana because no other Judges wanted this case because rumors of them losing their job was at risk." 'Is it true Judge?" I ask.

She sat there saying nothing in response as I didn't need an answer, her expression told me all I needed to know.

"Isn't this a private park and how did you get this to happen, its rumors that you deal with the crime underworld. Judge ask.

I said nothing at first.

"The owner is doing the city a favor and maybe he will make some pocket change." I said.

"He must have very large pockets." Judge said.

Her response told me that she has a sense of humor somewhere in that old wrinkle body as silence came between us noticing more and more coming.

"This was going to be a full house in no time and all Mayor." Judge said.

I could do was think of the profit I had coming from all direction when this is done.

"There a lot of entertainment going on and not to mention the celebrities." Judge said.

She was right, it look like every nationality in the world was right here, it was turning out ok so far and City Board voted against this believing it was going to be a disaster.

"Judge it looks like a red carpet event wouldn't you say?" I gestured.

"I'm glad that you're finding this very amusing Mayor, but I personally see nothing about this being funny and you made all of his happen right." *Judge ask.*

"It wasn't all me, so many had come to the city's aid Judge and all you see, it was them that made this possible. I explain.

"You know Mayor, you are very young to have such a responsibility and I hope you know what you're doing overall." 'You know the decision you make don't just affect the present but the future as well because this look more of a freak show especially with those half naked midget dancers." *Judge said.*

Chapter 27

Convoy

The sight of Mr. Whitfield could be seen from the distance, because of the high security and threats level.

"Judge were you aware that his dad posted a v25 million dollar reward for whom ever could get him back the United State." I said.

"I heard that your owned couldn't be trusted from the nemourios attempt to get him from your own system, don't you now have 5 Liberation Officers pending charges...I wouldn't want to be them." Judge said.

"There in protected custody of our Department of Defense Prison System. I said.

"It was rumored that he was been transported from Fredrick Douglass Army Base. Judge said.

I said nothing in response, maybe she was right even I wasn't always in the loop.

"Mayor, you have eyes in the sky." Judge said.

We could see the air support flying high, my only guess is that were for ground support.

"It nothing like a good show right Judge?" I ask.

"And what do you mean by that Mayor?" Judge ask

"Judge...look around, everyone here paid at least fifteen dollars to get in here to see the big show...this is an unforgettable moment in our history wouldn't you say judge?" And with that said Judge, they get to see me and best of all...you and who I believe is also a participant right." I ask.

147

"Mayor, can I call you by you first name because I have kids your age and the title you've should be upon someone older and more mature." Judge said.

"Judge, you may not...Mayor suit me just fine and with that being said...enjoy the show Judge, it's about to get real good!" I shouted.

Helicopters hovered.

"Judge, our military convoy is bringing in the guest of honor." I said laughing afterward.

"Yes it also seem like the policemen are having a hard time clearing that pathway from the dominantly white protestors." Judge said.

"I wouldn't be surprise if their all on Mr. Whitfield Sr payroll." I said loudly.

They were doing their best but it was just of many of them while our National Guard was holding back the black citizens.

"I bet they all came here to see Whitfield Jr get his ass beating like Toby." I said.

Something I must to have said caused the Judge to be hit with something, it didn't draw blood but it's the fact that someone had thrown something at her. Security rushed toward her, it wasn't long after, we had been removed from the area.

"Dam I thought we were safe around whities." I said jokingly.

We had been taking to the Trailer, it was there that we watch this become out of hand, several peoples had already been hurt and drag to the rear to get medical help while polices stood near to arresting the problem starter. I could do nothing but look on as we could see the policemen's using their dogs to make the crowd get back while the fire department move into position.

"It's this what you wanted Mayor, is this your decision and it hasn't even started and look at what is happen." "This was done to us and now you're doing it to them...how does it make you feel Mayor?" Judge ask.

I had said nothing while looking her way but I was thinking, shit its working from what I see.

"Judge it's amazing what a little high pressure water can really make a good widen path within seconds, you could bring a tank crew now." I said while laughing.

That moment Police Chief Jackson entered our area, he was totally wet as he turned on the big fan to dry off.

"This is my only uniform I brought, this wasn't supposed to happen." Chief Jackson said.

I made a joke of it as everyone laugh accept for the Judge who just gawked at us like if we were fools or something.

"Hey do you to want to sit with us, it better seats than ware you were?" Police Chief Jackson ask.

We could hear Chief Jackson radio.

"We gotten it under control Chief, we had to arrest several redneck trouble makers and taking a few more that look like trouble and the pathway should be open once the fireman get there hose's up Chief. Officer said.

Monitors showed everything while the helicopters hovered over while the military convoy waited patiently while seeing more vehicles unloading troops around the convoy. Maybe the judge was right about this getting out of control a little.

"Nothing good will come from this Mayor." Judge said.

"Hey, the more the merrier…safety comes with number right?" I said.

Some found it funny but others among us just look on, it had only taking a few minutes before the path was completely open and a few more arrest being made in the worst way involving medical attention for the arrestee.

"Judge, these fool didn't learn earlier from see their friends taking away and now them…peoples can be idiots. Don't you think Judge? I said.

"They are going to learn one way or the other." Judge said.

"That it Judge, that what I want to hear." I said loudly.

They don't run this country but white peoples no matter where they are, all love control and thinking they could do whatever they want. Some are realizing that this is not America…land of the white free and do as they please.

"Hey…Judge, with all the arrests been made, we may have to keep you around since it seem like we are going to have a lot more beating, sorry I meant business and with you harsh punishment tactics." 'I may have to speak with your District and keep you around a bit longer on temporarily assigned duty program." 'This could be an ongoing money

market, sorry I meant t to say...um- um- um, well you know what I mean Judge." I gestured.

The, Chief had insisted that we followed him after he dried off some.

"Just in time huh Judge." I ask.

The convoy just enter the main gate and with all that had happen.

"Look at all our kids are expose to Mayor, how do you feel about it and why didn't you put an age limit on this?" Judge ask.

"Why would I do that, they need to see this because maybe you want have to see them in your court room, wouldn't you agree Judge." I ask.

"So much blood Mayor, the fireman's are still spraying it into the grass just to clean it up." Judge said

We had taking our seats with the Chief Jackson.

"The view is amazing Chief Jackson, it like we on the 50 yard line for the big show wouldn't you agree Judge?" I ask.

Whomever designed this made me feel presidential inside, it was money well spent.

"Wow air conditioning and all Judge, I have to get me one of these no matter how much it cost the city Chief Jackson or you will be giving this one up to me." I said while laughing.

Chief Jackson didn't find it funny ass his old ass ignored me like if I was a kid or something.

"Enjoying the day so far Judge?" Chief Jackson ask.

"Yes I am Chief Jackson thanks for asking me." I said.

He said nothing as him and the Judge staring talking, it's was understandable since they were both almost older than dirt.

"Were you all around to hear Jesus on the mountain top?" I ask.

They didn't find it funny but I guess they do have lot to talk about like depends diaper and retirement and bengay and senior citizenship parking...old shit that involve their kind.

Chapter 28

The Seating

The crowed had become at a standstill the moment the military convoy stopped, it was like if it was something they never seen before.

"Judge...look there bringing the little bastard out in shackles like a slave straight from the mother land." I said.

His steps was slow like if he was heavily weighted down

"Judge this kid couldn't escape if he wanted to especially with the electronic monitors around his neck flashing like a fire alarm." I said

We watched him been escorted to the Metal Holding Facility, he was heavily guarded the entire time while the helicopters hovered above following him it seem.

"Judge there were many attempts alone with peoples boasting about what they was going to do to get him back home." I said.

"Not on my watch." Chief Jackson said.

"Not too bad for a country full off monkeys as Mr. Whitfield Sr said it." Someone said.

"So. What do you think Judge, is the show going pretty good for you so far?" I ask.

She said nothing but I knew what she was thinking as several young peoples had made their way toward us wanting to take pictures as I didn't mind myself but the Judge was hesitant and very unfriendly to sum it up. I never known that my life was to be in the celebrity status but I guest time has a way of making you know who you're or what you're destine to become.

"You know that you could still stop this don't you mayor." Judge said.

"And not give you the opportunity to not get yours in judge, now wouldn't that be fair knowing you have been a part of this from day one and now you're about to become part of the spotlight yourself judge.

She just look my way before glancing at the sound of the crowed going crazy, it was Whitfield Jr being escorted. He walked freely but still being heavily guarded like if he was an escape felon as they took him to the *Medical Examiner Tyince.*

"What you see is proto call before the punishment can be giving, but it is still your overall say so Mayor." Judge said.

It didn't take long before they had gave him approval as we watch the *Medical Examiner Tyince* make her way toward me. Cameras followed her the entire time as she now stood before me.

"This is the medical exam and it required your signature Mayor."

"Mayor, all eyes are on you." Charnel said.

She was right when I took notice of it.

"I must give them a show then." I said.

"Don't do it." Charnel said.

I stood up looking at Whitfield Jr before making my way toward him from this glass capsule.

"Do you understand why you are here son?" I ask.

He stood there looking at me saying nothing until I asked him again after I placed my hand on his shoulder only to have him move away from me aggressively.

"Go f*ck yourself." Whitfield Jr said loudly.

"What did you just tell me?" I asked.

"Go f*ck your mommy monkey and after you're done, crawl back inside that black hole and die, you think my dad is going to let you put one hand on me in this land of monkeys." Whitfield Jr. shouted loudly.

It was that moment after he spit in my eyes and the sight of his dad been held back by the Security when he tried to come from his assigned area.

"I'm going to signed this you little disrespectful blue eyed bastard."
I said loudly.

Medical Examiner Tyince had giving me several antiseptic wipes, I watched him smile like if he didn't just spit in my eye.

"Son, I hope they beat your ass so bad until your skin peel from your own worthless body." I said.

The protestors booed none stop.

"Was that necessary Mayor." Judge ask.

Judge was very opinionated as I receive my rum and cola.

"This isn't the place to be drinking like a fish." Charnel said.

I said nothing back as I started drinking knowing she was going to make this a long day and I needed to relax me.

"Doesn't he look smaller to you Mayor" Judge ask.

I taking a second look at him.

"Little bastard is smaller than before, maybe he didn't find his cuisine appetizing, it's his choice if he refuse to eat."

"He was about 225 when he stood before me." Mayor said.

"Little rich bastard should have too many choices in life, he should've gotten shanked or something." I said.

"You know we have two of his cousins now in custody." Judge said.

"I will never understand rich peoples, they came to see him and that night both of them gotten arrested for almost the same crap." I said.

Chapter 29

Mr. Whitfield Jr. Introduction

Announcer had come over the sound power his voiced echoed throughout the entire park over the loudness.

"Mr. Whitfield Jr." 'You've been found guilty of several violations within the City of Liberation for physically assaulting an Officer and two violation of sexual assault, one involving physically penetration with your hands underneath her clothing." 'You enter a night club with false identification that resulted in underage drinking causing you to be drunk in and outside of the club...public intoxication." 'Mr. Whitfield Jr. you have been sentence to public punishment, is there anything you want to say before this is carried out?" Announcer ask.

We watched him stand their guarded as they brought him the microphone, he stood there looking around before turning toward his family.

"Dad get me away from these black dumbass land of monkeys!" Whitfield Jr. yelled his loudest.

The sight of everyone was at an up roar, the black citizen yelling in anger while the white cheered him on.

"This was not going to be good Mayor." Judge said.

Authority personnel had done their best to keep both nationality apart, there was so much hostility going on.

"I hope this doesn't become a riot Judge, we didn't have enough personnel to keep this completely under control if they do get to acting a fool." I said

"What are you checking?" Judge ask.

I said nothing but I had a helicopter on standby just in case, you can never be too sure about this type of event.

"Mr. Whitfield…what you just done was nothing more than an insult to this entire justice system and you may face more prosecution once this is done." 'As far as now…order of the Superior Municipal Court of Liberation you are to be face punished for the laws you have violated and it's to be giving immediate…signed by the Mayor himself only minutes ago." 'Along with the Chief Medical Examiner Tyince that you're fit and healthy to receive 3 flog for each crime committed and time two for spitting and insulting a Superior Judge representing the County of Liberation and State of Texas." Announcer said loudly

We could do nothing but watch Billy Bad Ass.

"His daddy has no control in this country Judge, I'm glad he brought his family to see his punk ass son about to get a proper beat down." I said.

"You could stop this Mayor." Judge said.

"There was no amount of money going to save his lily white-ass from receiving this beating he had coming his way Judge." I said.

"Mr. Whitfield Jr., this punishment will be giving in stages and each flog giving will be examined according to the State of Texas Punishment Review Board and it will be up to the Medical Examiner Tyince decision if this is to continued or you've the right to stop this at any time but if you chose to do so." 'You must be advise before and after that you will remain in our custody until you are able to begin from the beginning with State Medical Approval."

"Does it always takes this long Judge?" I ask.

She look my way before going back to sipping on her none alcoholic lemon tea, what a waste of a good hearty ice filled drink with real lemon floating.

"Mr. Whitfield there will be 6 Certified License Punisher assigned to this Public Punishing, three males and three females." 'Each one will be drawn from this hand turned machine by a certified personnel alone with the weapons and area of the body in which." 'You shall receive the punishment according to the number drawn, in the event that something doesn't work." 'It will become physical until it shall be put back into working condition." Announcer said.

We watched the *Announcer* take another look at his paper work, im sure he knew it like the back of his hand from doing it so much.

"Judge all the Executioners are black out from head to toe, it like they are out of some mid-evil movie." I said.

They stood like monster especially the giant one, his 300lbs 6ft6 sized alone could hurt someone easy. This man could have been an athlete's but this was also very competitive in getting work, it was a dog eat dog if you wanted an on-going paycheck.

"Judge do you know any of them." I ask.

She ignored me as I just laughed.

"Mr. Whitfield Jr. we're are going to remove your clothing and the Medical Examiner Tyince Team is going to get you ready to receive your punishment." Announcer said.

Cameras zoomed in, it was like if it was personnel by the way they force him to his feet's when he refuse to stand.

"Judge look at Mr. Badass struggling to keep his cloth on." I said.

It had taking them a moment to strip him of his orange jump suit.

"Pink and white strip diaper...told you he was a b*tch Judge." I said

"That not funny, it's meant for embarrassment Mayor and that commit was un-call for." Judge said.

Cameras flashed none stop while he call for his mommy and dad while the monitors displayed them along with his family.

"Judge they are in for a really good show." I said.

Judge shook her head.

"Mr. Whitfield you must stand." Medical Examiner Tyince explained why.

They had to force him up while the *Announcer* now look at the *Medical Examiner Tyince* giving thumbs up.

"Mr. Whitfield you are subject to five body parts and once the wheel is spent, it will be giving and so on." Announcer said.

It was that moment as we watch the wheel turning, the sight of several balls could be seen until it stopped. Medical Examiner Tyince had taking control of those from the dispenser, she read them over the sound power system, her voice was loud and clear.

"Mr. Whitfield Jr." "You are to be giving 2 flogging to the buttock area and it will be administered immediately." Medical Examiner Tyince explained.

The minute he had heard that, he had begun moving about crazily but there was no where he could go as we watch the *Executioner #.He* could do nothing but look at him shaking his head, protestors shouted loudly. "Judge their dragging the trouble makers away." I said.

"Hopefully it will calm the rest down," Judge responded.

The way they were yelling while bleeding, it had to become effective eventually because there wasn't no more warning.

"What you think of that Judge?" She just look shaking her head while mumbling something like animals.

Mr. Whitfield continued fighting, it would've been easier if he would have just stood there and follow instruction but he didn't. *Medical Examiner Tyince* tried to come him down but it done no good the *Over Watched Panel* decided to have a device that was designed to assist.

"That device is nothing more than mad scientist creation." Judge said.

Several guards were rolling it toward him, it gotten everyone attention.

"I have seen this device used a few times and there is nothing human about it, it should be out lawed." Judge said angrily.

It wasn't an easy device to look upon, its leather strapped made it look creepy along with the way it folded as they braced him into this contraption no matter how much he fought to keep from being restrained.

"Judge he look like he had been in some severe accident." I said.

The rusty look didn't help, it told the world that we can't even maintain our own equipment, you could even here the nuts and bolt grinding against each other.

"I can't believe it take four peoples to get him ready." Chief Jackson said loudly.

Medical Examiner Tyince had taking one last look before giving the ok, he continue to breathe harder from the way he struggled it seem.

"Judge how long it takes to get this beating on." I ask.

"You have somewhere you have to be Mayor." Judge ask.

"He should have just bent his ass over." I said.

"I don't think they know how to operate the mechanical hydraulic contraption mechanism Mayor. Judge said.

They kept playing with the controls, they couldn't get his body position right it seems, Whitfield Jr looked so uncomfortable.

"Judge do you see the way his family is looking on, maybe it was the tear rolling down his face and there was nothing his family could do." I said.

"Whitfield mom is crying even while her husband is holding her." Judge said.

Cameras zoomed in on them, there was no privacy among this place, their eyes gotten bigger when one of the *Medical Personal* walked over and pull down the diaper type flap.

"His bare ass is expose to the world Judge." I said laughing.

Protestors roar out loud in anger while the other cheered it on knowing what about to happen while the Comedians were making gay jokes none stop.

"Maybe they should let the Executioners give him some deep penetration to his ass one after another." I said.

"Please grow up Mayor." Judge said.

"Judge you didn't find that hairy ass joke funny about Whitfield Jr, he really did need a barber right about now." I said.

They finally gotten him ready.

"You're going to be sprayed with a pepper type oily chemical made to it heal and induce the pain as well." Medical Examiner Tyince said.

We watch one of her team walked toward Mr. Whitfield Jr. slowly and sprayed his buttock area, we could tell that its burned him from first contact by the way he keep wiggling his ass around. The way he moved, it was as if we all felt his pain, cameras showed how it even stuck to ass hair while rolling down his crack to his big pink dangling balls.

"They could have least covered them up or something, it just ruined my appetite for my meatballs…I was just about to eat." Comedian Sam said.

"This was definitely not for the kids but maybe it's an eye open for them, wouldn't you say Judge, better they learn now then to be standing before you right?" Chief Jackson said loudly.

Chapter 30

Whitfield Jr. Punishment

That moment the *Announcer* gave the order to spin the wheel, a florescent ball appeared in the dispenser as we watch the *Medical Examiner Tyince* taking it. She stood there looking at it as we could only imagine what it said. The crowed gotten quiet as she placed it back in an awaiting basket after reading it to us. *Executioner* came forward reaching for the wooden paddle lined with many shiny metal holes in between.

"Stop it...don't do this...im sorry for whatever I done to cause... im so sorry...please stop." Whitfield Jr begged.

We could hear him calling for his daddy, this Mr. Bad Ass yelled even louder when the *Executioner* was making his way slowly to him like a veteran.

"Whomever this is Judge, he seem to be in no rush or anything." I said.

He stood directly in front of Whitfield Jr waving the paddle in his face, this was nothing more than taunting him before whopping his ass. Whitfield Jr said something but we couldn't hear, but im sure it was more begging as the *Executioner* moved behind the kid.

"He gotten his stance down to a science Judge." I said.

He swung from thin air so hard that Whitfield Jr cried out loud.

"That kid ass is feeling some real pain Judge," I said.

Whatever this poorly man made contraption was, it vibrated giving off the worst sounds like if it was going to fall apart. Whitfield Jr body shook, this was nothing but pain from the way his red ass jiggle like jelly.

"Tears huh Mayor, you're so new to this aren't you?" Judge ask.

I said nothing but looked at her way while wiping my face before the camera caught me as the *Executioner* tried to remove the paddle his from bloody ass now. Camera zoomed in so good that you could see flesh jam into the holes of the wooden paddle.

"Wow do you hear this crowed Judge cheering while others gotten louder." I asked.

Whitfield Jr screamed to the top of his voice, it echoed through this entire park, this was nothing but money in the making. *Medical Examiner Tyince* had made her way to see what was going on, his ass really was stuck.

"Judge, he only has 23 to go, do you think he will be man enough to continue?" I ask.

Judge said nothing back.

"Mr. Whitfield Jr we've a problem and I'm going to pour this antiseptic that is design to clean and loosening the sticky oil." Medical Examiner Tyince explain.

Cameras zooming in while the paddle was slowly being pull from his ass, it wasn't long after that thumbs up being giving. *Executioner* moved in closer like if he was coming up to bat ignoring the loudness. He had taking a second to look before placing the paddle between his legs while rubbing loose dirt in his hands. Some cheered when the *Medical Examiner Tyince* sprayed his ass, his movement told everyone it burn deeply from the way his ass was twitching like if he was getting ram deeply.

"Judge the best part of this is seeing his ass lock into that crummy brace while he search for anything he could grab but there was nothing. I said.

Silence came upon the n*ggas but the white protestors gotten louder while the Comedians were making jokes about the *Executioner* getting the right stance. That when the n*ggas cheered when the paddle had been raised. We thought he was going to swing from the opposite direction but he didn't this time, maybe he twisted his arm earlier...Whitfield Jr yell even louder than before. It was that moment the *Executioner* lowered his paddle looking at the *Medical Examiner Tyince* that force the *Executioner* away to his seating area.

"Judge what the hell is he doing ruining the show like this, why is he sitting down?" I ask.

Whitefield Jr had words with the *Medical Examiner Tyince*, it was that moment she told him.

"That if he don't stop the yelling he was going to be gage" Medical **Examiner Tyince explained.**

Wow is all I could think, this *Executioner* needed silence to beat someone ass, this was some truly out of this world amazing shit happening before my face.

"Go f*ck yourself you black nappy head nigger monkey b*tch!" **Whitfield Jr. yell his loudest.**

Wow, everyone heard that loud and clear, the protestors cheered him on while the black citizen didn't find it funny. You could hear the black women yelling about what he just said, he wasn't on their favorite list after that commit.

"Whitfield Jr may never be able to go back to the hood and buy **some jungle after that commit, I bet and if he did, it would have to be** **more than the going rate." Comedian Sam said.**

Sam had some major psychological issues.

"Executioner, he is all your!" Medical Examiner Tyince yell loudly.

That second he had been bent back into position by the *Guards* while the *Executioner* had taking his last bite from his sandwich. If no one knew what he was before, we could all tell from those big black Wesley looking lips as he pull the hood back over his blackness.

"Hey, you think he will give me the remainder of his lunch Jim." **Comedian Sam ask.**

His heavily stained greasy brown bag he placed in some dingy looking metal cooler must to have giving him this burst of energy.

"Judge did you see the way he moved like flies on shit to Whitfield **Jr or maybe it was those racial words or maybe it was personal now."** **'What you think?" I ask.**

The way he rubbed dirt once more.

"Well he want be yelling no more Judge." I said.

Some sort of orange ball had been shoved in his mouth as we watched the Medical Examiner Tyince personally tied the leather straps herself.

"It looks like he didn't enjoy that from the way he tried to fight **Judge." I said.**

Executioner moved behind him slowly tapping that ass while searching for the right angle from a left handed swinging position. He brought the paddle even higher than last time while he slightly moved his left foot for better gripping I guess.

"He should've lots of energy from the 3 pork fatback chitlin pork deep fried barbecue sandwiches we all saw him devour one after another." Comedian Sam said.

"So how about you Jim, do you think he pull something like a muscle or something while he spoke about how the others Executioners was stretching really well?" "You think it was the n.i.g.g.e.r words Jim and did you see the way they huddle before he left like if they were playing football." Comedian Sam ask.

"Maybe they are a team and not just strangers." Comedian Thomas said.

"Yea, he is…let's wave!" Comedian Sam responded.

"Now that just rude." Comedian Thomas said.

"What the hell did he just call time out?" Comedian Sam ask.

"Yes he did but we've a radio shout out from Weave Nappy Heads Be Gone from the World of Nappy Heads…We Are You and they have this new Section 8 slash rent program to where you can pay daily and weekly this is only a radio commercial and now back to you Thomas and not directly from me because I want to leaves from here in peace. Comedian Sam shouted laughing afterward.

"All I could say was wow."

Announcer had shouted out to everyone that a local band call the… "*Broke Ass Niggas*"…will be performing their newest song call…*Getting that Booty* and Smacking *that Ass n Sweating Balls* will follow. It wasn't bad as I watch them perform, they even had half naked girls walking around collecting money with basket, like if this was church or something. This was some real n*gga shit before our faces.

"So, Thomas what is your opinion." Comedian Sam ask.

"Like you, I want to go home to." Comedian Thomas said.

"Well it look like he is better now Thomas." Comedian Sam ask.

The sight of his swing was so hard that it broken the paddle handle while the other half was glued to Whitfield Jr ass. The crowed was at an up roar, you could see the *Police* getting a little nervous themselves while the *Military* had begun taking control of the trouble makers. The comedians never seen to stop making jokes about Whitfield Jr ass but this wasn't the time, there was already enough hostility.

"So, Judge how many of these have you seen this close and personal?"
I ask.

"More that I care to you remember Mayor, you seem to be like a kid in a candy store…it seem like you're having too much fun, but let chat about you and what you're searching for." 'So, you sat with the American President, how was that for you?" 'And what was he like…was this your opportunity to play major politic world. Judge asked.

I had to explain that I was nothing more than a guest of our own President and Governor.

"It would hard for me to believe that you of all peoples sat in silence without a word and are you wanting the big seat?" Judge ask.

"Why would you ask that Judge?" I ask.

"Look around Mayor, this kid was supposed to be home by now and somehow you pushed this forward, is it because you want the fame that follows?" 'This alone has made your name well known wouldn't you say?" Judge ask.

I sat there looking at her talk more about how it's in my eyes alone with greed and none pity for others, this old hag was talking to me like if I was her child or something.

"You know Mayor, I myself play with enough lives under the name of justice but you don't seem to be on the side of justice or fairness." Judge said.

I'm the guilty one according to her old wrinkle ass, this little bastard slapped one of my Officers and I'm supposed to just let him walk away.

"That young man broken the law and if it takes guts from me not be afraid of Mr. Plantation America, than don't that say a lot about who I'm and what I stand for Judge and what about you, you made this happen." I said.

"You know you can stop this and pardon him before this gets any worse and from looking at the protestors Mayor, you're not building friends but the opposite…don't you see." Judge said.

I said nothing back at first because, she was like talking to the air.

"Judge listen, deep down inside of me…there a part that don't give a shit about this kid or the white who only stayed here because

America grandfathered them land plus monthly financial assistance."
I said aggressively.

It was that moment, the show gotten back on the road.

"Mr. Whitfield you've accepted 2 flogging and I must ask you if
you can continue." Medical Examiner Tyince ask.

We watched this fool looked her way and calling her out of her name
after looking his daddy way.

"That sound like a yes to me." Medical Examiner Tyince said.

She look toward the *Announcer* giving him the ok to proceed.

"Mayor you have lots of anger, does seeing this kid make you even
angrier." Judge ask.

"No…richer Judge." I responded.

Camera zoomed in on the florescent ball coming for the dispenser as
the *Medical Examiner Tyince* had taking it.

"You are too receive 3 floggings on the bottom of both feet's Mr.
Whitfield Jr." She said.

This had to be the worse but the when I spoke to the Judge, she taking
one look at me.

"What do I know about it Mayor?" Judge ask.

"What an old b*tch." I mumbled to myself.

I knew she saw the movement of my lips as I took several more drinks
to relax, she was only a word away before I put her in her old wrinkle up
place. Maybe we shouldn't be sitting together, we are just too different as
we watch them unstrapping him from that contraption but the second
he had been freed, all you could see was his red white bare ass jiggling.
Whitfield Jr was running like a slave for his freedom but they gotten him
within a few seconds easily. There was nowhere for him to go.

"There're going to have to strap him in." Judge said.

It didn't take a rocket scientist to figure that out from the way they had
to wrestle in down, you could see his family standing up. If they would've
taught him better, they wouldn't be here but good they didn't as I could
only estimate the money I had coming my way from this.

"So, judge have you ever seen that before." I ask.

She didn't even respond, the thought of her choking on that pig feet
she was tearing to pieces would have giving another show.

"He is really going to get it now isn't he Thomas, maybe even like Konta right Thomas?" Comedian Sam said.

Protestors gotten loud but crowed control move in quickly knowing all it takes it one to cause an out of control up roar.

"Those two clowns are going to be jobless if they keep making crazy commits especially Sam, he seem to be a racist." Judge said.

Whitfield Jr gotten strapped back into the rusty looking chair, it was another poorly maintain piece of crap made by another mad scientist, maybe the same one. His legs was strap together while his arms rested flat while he could see the entire thing from the way he sat up right. I could only hope the youth was getting an eyes full, this shit look like it was going to hurt.

"I hate to be him Judge" I said.

Executioner 3 had been chosen to performing this punishment, it had to have been a woman from her small frame. She had gotten the leather looking stick, it was something out of medieval time it seem but maybe he was in luck. She didn't look like she could do much damage as she moved forward slowly cutting the air, it sounded like hissing before it came to a stop. She had done this several times while his feet's was been sprayed.

"You may proceed." Medical Examiner Tyince said while moving out the way.

Executioner walk several times around him like if it was personal from the way she was looking at him. That moment she had stopped in front of him.

"She is really going to enjoy this too much Judge." I said.

Entire crowed became silent, she move slightly before swinging putting the sun on her back causing him to jump but she only getting her distance.

"Judge is this normal?" I ask.

"Didn't you want a good show Mayor?" Judge responded.

"I guess I did Judge." I said.

"Mayor are you aware of how this gotten started." Judge said.

"Over crowed prison." I responded.

"Mayor it started several years after this country establishment and we were actually making cells out of metal storage units." 'We didn't have the money to keep building prisons and that how this was form." Judge said.

"I guess beating ass Judge, our inmate population is kept to a minimum." I said.

That moment she swung with one hand out for balance and the other almost behind her back. You could hear the air been cut just before she made contact, my owned eyes water. Cameras caught the crowed facial expression, it was as if they felt all 12 whips wrapping around his feet's in slow motion. Impact alone tore into his flesh, you could see blood.

"Judge, look at that nappy headed camera man with the red and green pick fork coming from his hair, would you've thought he had such skills to zoom in at catch such good footage?" I said.

The sound of Whitfield Jr hollering his loudest while they zoomed in on his mom crying for her b*tch of son.

"Judge would you say the show is good so far." I ask.

"This is becoming very emotional, the cameras is showing so much sadness on the monitors." Judge said.

Medical Examiner Tyince look at him once again before giving the Executioner thumbs up as she gotten her distance once more.

"Ding-Dong." Comedian sounded.

It gotten the protestors fired up while the other half cheered even louder.

"Thomas do you think Mr. Whitfield Sr is paying these protestor?" Comedian Sam ask.

"Maybe but he would've to pay me even more to cause a ruckus and get my ass beat, he definitely have the money to make it happen. Comedian Thomas said.

"You could be right about that Thomas and how come you didn't have your peeps to bring me some cool-aid and fried baloney sandwich and watermelon, since you haven't offered." 'You know you've everything accept pigging feet's and deep fried chicken." Sam said laughing afterwards.

"Sam, look around, you ain't black and this ain't America, I don't think you are very well like judging from how everyone is looking up at us.

"Sorry my broke brothers and hoodrat sisters and fatherless children's." Comedian Sam said looking at the crowed that was mad dogging him even more now.

"Sam, you know your buddies the Klan Head Quarters moved back to America and I see no white sheets out there supporting you here." Comedian Thomas said loudly while scooting away from him.

It was that moment the *Executioner* reposition herself to the other side after a few practice swings.

"Did you see the way that little bastard jump when she made contact." I said.

We could see tiny pieces of metal strips in the leather from the zooming camera. That alone was maybe why he yell over power the band when they pull it from his ass.

"Thomas how can you sit and salted down that watermelon and not offer me a bite of that high blood pressure?" Comedian Sam ask.

"Sam is it's it true you got exile from America, im sure, we would all like to know why you're really here with us monkeys." Thomas ask.

"Long story Thomas, very long story and I never told anyone... just making it clear and to completely answer your question, it was 3 slashes...see." Comedian Sam shown him the love from this country.

"Must to have been some good public sex you gave her, you know we have sanction places for that kind of behavior right." Thomas said over the sound system exposing his friend's life.

"From the way you're smiling Thomas, you do look in need of a woman to rid you of that horney-ness look upon your face." Comedian Sam said.

"Hey, enough of me and I don't want to hear nothing else of your gay-ness Sam...TMI-TMI, let's talk about the Whitfield kid now. Comedian Thomas yell while moving farther from him.

"Hey you know I can still feel him sometimes." Comedian Sam said loudly."

"Did you hear those two fools letting the world know about their gayness?" I ask.

Thomas was yelling TMI-TMI repeatedly while parents was covering up their kids ears.

"It was over 2 years ago." Sam said.

"I had enough of these two myself." Judge said.

Mr. Whitfield Jr had one more to go as he refuse water from the Medics.

"All of you monkey can get the hell out of his face." Whitfield Jr yelled.

We could tell that he wanted this over, his protestors heard every word while his voice echoed throughout the park spreading like a wild fire. So much aggression from both sides…maybe it excited him as well.

"Hey, Judge…were did he get some balls from?" I ask.

Security had force his family to sit back down, the protestor had become louder while the comedians joked of how she position herself once more before striking like a viper without warning. Forcing him to cry out but it wasn't as loud as before but he felt it.

"Is that all you monkey got!" Whitfield yelled his loudest at everyone after denying water again knocking it from the Medic hand.

Chapter 31

"Who Is Next?"

Whitfield Jr look at the *Announcer*

"Hurry up, you bastards can't hurt me and show yourselves you cowards." Whitfield Jr yelled.

This kid was really asking for it yelling.

"Who is next?" Whitfield Jr continue yelling.

He yelled at *Guards* to get back as they tried to calm him down, so he could be examined.

"Judge do you see this arrogance bastard, is this normal or what?" I ask.

"The world will see how he can take it and more and he may become immortal, when this is all said and done." Judge said.

Maybe she is right as we watch him been force back down, that moment he had been unstrapped and giving sandals. The sight of him throwing them toward the *Executioner*, this was nothing more than disrespect, even more so when he looked at us.

"F*ck all you black monkeys in this waste land you call a country!" Whitfield Jr shouted loudly.

This kid was really is an idiot is all I could say, his words was barely heard but the cameras zoom in on his facial expression, it told the story altogether. Whitfield Jr was driving his protestors crazy with his none sense but in reality. It only made the show better as we waited to see what was going to be call and I wanted nothing more than for him to feel his back explode. I wanted to see something big that was going to inflict nothing but pain, the *Executioner* who sat patiently waiting had stood up very aggressive. It wasn't just him that looked pissed but everyone in his circle shared that same look.

"Dammit!" I shouted.

The…Judge looked my way, she wanted to know what was on my mind from the way I shouted out.

"I really wanted the giant to be in on this." I said.

Judge had done nothing but shook her head looking at the small size *Executioner* making his or her big day view. Whomever it was had been instructed to pick up a set a bamboo metal laced canes.

"You may only use them once and after use, it must be separated from original stack." Announcer explained.

Those ass clowns comedians was stealing her spotlight while Whitfield Jr had chosen to take it like a man. We all had no idea what fire got lite under his ass but all sudden he developed a pair of balls. I can only imagine how long it would last, once they really get into that ass.

"I've only encountered this type of punishment only few times and he is better off using the chest support brace." Judge said.

We could see the *Medical Team* given the okay after checking him out, the moment the *Executioner* was about to move his direction he or she had been stopped.

"What the hell are they doing Judge?" I ask.

"This is a first, this has become personal I think and they want him to feel every slash." Judge said.

Executioner had been given approval minutes later, the sound alone was horrifying, the way it made contact with Whitfield Jr. I would've died from the pain and knowing I had 19 more to go and the way he denied his sandals, this fool knock them from one of the *Medics* hands.

"Judge did you see the way he just showed his ass?" I asked.

The protesters gotten hype from the what he just done, not to mention how he was barely able to stand told us how much pain he was in from the way he moving.

"Judge do you think it burned the way they say it does?" I asked.

"That oily spray is designed to heal but it burns at the same time Mayor, you should try it." Judge said.

The longer he stood on his feet, the more it penetrated his flesh as he stood there watching the *Executioner*. Both form this hostile relationship and his bravery was nothing more than his ignorance. *Executioner* waive to the *Medic*, the sight of him being sprayed with this oily spray. Whitfield Jr had been surprise, the *Executioner* didn't even give the *Medic* time to return to give the final approval.

It happened in the blink of an eye, the sound alone was like a teacher hitting the chalkboard with a ruler without warning. Whitfield Jr had been hit so hard it caused me to cringe up.

"Wow that Executioners is heartless Judge, see how he caused the protesters to uproar." I said.

Comedians only gotten more fuel to add to this existing fire of Whitfield Jr been in some serious pain his back turned bloody red while the cameras zoomed in on what was happening.

"You are nothing, this is all you monkeys got for me!" Whitfield Jr yell afterwards.

Executioner flung the cane down on the ground was nothing but madness and aggression, he had chosen another while the *Medic* was doing what she could to help. Whitfield Jr had done nothing but push her away.

"Is that all you got…you are nothing!" Mr. Whitfield yell to the Executioner.

This was turning out to be a war, the *Executioner* slammed into Whitfield Jr once more only seconds after the *Medical Personnel* has stepped aside. We watch him break down in pain but not once did he cry or scream out as he did before.

"You will all suffer, this country of monkey shit will pay dearly… that I promise! Whitfield Jr yell even louder.

His laughter could be heard loudly but we knew he was in more pain that he ever wanted while pushing the *Medical Team* away, the camera caught him looking towards his family. Expression of pain and yet insanity as if nothing was hurting him. It was freaky.

"Is this all you have for me…you monkeys can do better than this, you're all worthless uneducated pieces of what this country is…shit!" Whitfield Jr yell directly into the cameras with fear of nothing.

This little rich bastard should be breaking down but he was getting stronger as he waved to the *Executioner*.

"Hey…Ape…come and finish making your pennies an hour!" *Whitfield Jr shouted."*

It alone was like a knocking down like a prize fighter, the sight alone had exploded the *Executioner* as Whitfield Jr never taking his eyes while being forced into his stance grinning. We could all see that his back was covered in blood from the way each cane sliced into his flesh cutting him deeply. I couldn't even imagine where his mind was knowing what was about to happen, maybe he was in a world that no one could touch as he didn't even move this time. His body had taken all that the *Executioner* had given him and yet he stood tall without making a sound after the pain had been inflicted upon him.

"Judge what is going on here, he should be begging for us to stop this by now." *I asked.*

It's like he can barely move now."

"Well, this is the show you wanted right, he has figured out what you've done and he is not giving you the satisfaction or I should say us." *'Because this country represent us as a functional nation, this young man will die before he shows you anymore weakness."* *Judge explained.*

"Maybe he will, I'm getting a show and now I've his cousin." *I said while thinking maybe a bigger payday.*

"What does that mean Mayor?" *Judge ask.*

I looked at her knowing that I shouldn't have said it out of angry but she just sat there looking like my grandmother would.

"What done in the dark has a way of finding the light and you should be careful of the things you do behind closed doors." *Judge said calmly.*

I has said nothing back noticing the wrinkly looking *Sheriff* who seem to be listening to every spoken word between us.

"May I help you Sheriff." *I ask.*

He said nothing back while never taking his eyes from me munching on a pig feet in one hand and ham hock in the other. I could only hope that he is eaten his death from the high blood pressure he destined to receive as I turned away too concentrated on the kid now. The sight of *Executioner* standing there hoping Whitfield Jr want make it through this flogging.

"Mayor, he has one more cane left. Judge said.

We watch him take it from the basket, before the *Examiner* could even take a look at him, *Executioner* tore into this kid ass like if he was a step child.

"He may lose his license for what he just done." Judge said.

I don't know much about the rules and regulations but I suppose you can't hit someone directly in the spinal cord. *Announcer* was having a field day with this as we watched the *Executioner* been taken away by *Guards*. Whitfield Jr had found himself on his knees feeling like shit I'm sure, this kid was in some serious pain.

"You know you could pardon him and this will be done with." *Mayor suggested.*

"Well…Judge as much as I would like to, what kind of man I would be to give these good peoples who has travel so far to see a good show." 'Anything but less. I replied.

I wanted to see this little rich blue eyed bastard break, even if they had to carry him away in an ambulance, it would be to my satisfaction as well as those who come to see him get beat like a stepchild. The protesters was at an up rage as a *Military* had to step in arresting agitators looking to make a race riot out of this. Whitfield continue been ignorant by pushing the *Medics* away as he gotten up on his own. His words had been silence due to his beat-down moment ago.

"You know this Executioner can be held liable for any major injuries." Judge said.

"Well…Judge you can't get water from empty glass…those guys are competing and traveling out of their own pocket just to get work. I said.

She said nothing more only because she knew I was right, most of these guys are ex-felons themselves and criminals of the worst with the lowest of education.

"How much experience do you have to have to learn to beat some ass Judge?" I ask.

This kid wasn't smart, he was nothing more than an idiot but I guess money can do that to people sometimes as he look towards *Executioners* and laugh. The comedians made jokes out of it that had everyone laughing, they were idiots as well. The wheel had been spent, he was to receive 3 flogging on his upper rear legs to be given by *Executioner 2*.

"I'm pulling my authority and you will be giving the comfort of our padded leather bed." Medical Examiner Tyince explained.

We watched the Guards bring it out.

"You know that is a very sensitive area of the body but highly effective way of receiving your punishment." Judge said.

Mr. Whitfield Jr refuse the leathery mouthpiece alone with the bed, both was for his own protection and this kid had too much attitude for his own good. He stood there strong and tall while concentrating on his balance as he was being sprayed, the oily chemical could be seen running down the back of his legs. *Executioner* demeanor told us that he was a man with a low tolerance for ignorance from the way he swung that leather strap around.

"That device should be outlawed." Judge said.

He held the wooden handle tightly as I could see why it should've been outlawed, those four leather strips look like pieces of Santa belt with small pieces of metal.

"You know nothing makes contact like that thing burying itself into your flash one after another." Judge said.

"Really." I said.

"It doesn't matter how tough you think you're that strap is known as the Devils belt and it will put you on the ground." Judge said.

Executioner move-in behind him the second he had been given the go-ahead from the *Medical Examiner Tyince*. It happened so quickly that I didn't even see it, but the sight of him on the ground looking around like what the hell just happen. He move slowly until he gotten on his knees without help and eventually back on his feet's. The crowd must to have felt so bad for him that they cheer especially when he wave the *Medics* away once again looking at the *Executioner* laughing.

"What the hell is this kid on Judge?" I ask.

She said nothing as she looked my way for a brief second as he stood there with the devils belt in his hand moving it about. The long wide strap dangle just before he swung again, the cameras zoom in once it made contact with his flesh. His family eyes widen while tears poured down there face, you could see his dad yelling while being forced to sit back down. It was that moment that he just laid there, his legs was jumping like a lizard tail that just been cut off and yet, he never made a crying sound.

The sight alone terrified the kids while parents held their hands over their kid's eyes, so many cameras from around the world never stop flashing. The judge was doing nothing more than shaking her head while tears could be seen coming from her eyes.

"Why do you even care, you seen so much of this Judge?" I ask.

She said nothing back but then again I had to think that she was also a mother, it had taken him a moment to just get back to his knees this time as we watch him grab the back of his legs doing what he could to get back to his feet's. I could hear one of the comedians joking, he was doing his best to get people to laugh to take away the sadness of him struggling. Devil belt is no joke.

"Hey Thomas, are those tears in your eyes?" 'You know Thomas I was wondering if I could call you Tom like in Uncle Tom." 'Would you mind since we're friends and all and do you know I've a cabin?" Comedian Sam laughed while Thomas looked at him like a fool.

It had taken him longer to get back to his feet's as he stood there on one knee breathing heavy while the *Medical Staff* tried to help him knowing she didn't have the power to stop it, only with his permission. Most inmates would just want to get it over with and I think that's what he was trying to do. It wasn't long after she had given thumbs up as they spent the wheel, it was the blue ball.

"That's rare." Judge said.

Chapter 32

The Break

I've been told by the judge that it had been added for many reasons but it was to be given after his medical attention. Whitfield Jr had no say so, I myself didn't realize how fast time had gone by as we watched him being taken away. He really needed it from all that has happened.

"Don't you think, you should go see him?" Judge ask.

"Why?" I responded.

It was that moment, she had just look at me before getting up walking away looking back at me stopping.

"Well...aren't you coming Mayor?"

I had no intention but it was the only right thing to do as I gotten up only to arrive, the sight of Whitfield Jr lying there in his own blood expelling from his mutilated body as I stood back while the judge moved towards him. His family wasn't impress with none of us, it was like they wanted nothing more than for us not to be a part of their family time.

"Maybe we should just leave Judge." I said in a low tone of voice.

"Yea, that the best thing I heard all day monkey, in fact all you n*ggers should get the f*ck out." Whitfield Jr said with deep aggression yet barely talking.

This little bastard had no problem telling us what was on his mind and there was nothing any of us could do but stand there and look at him before leaving.

"Was going to see him worth it Judge?" I ask.

I started laughing, it was funny to me in so many ways.

"Whitfield are all nothing more than racist's pieces of shit Judge."
I said.

The moment I gotten back to my seat, it was nothing more than a blessing as I ordered several drinks, the judge just look on saying nothing. The contraption they brought out was nothing more than some homemade torture device. It should be used on terrorists, this thing was designed to release water.

"I know of this system, it should be outlawed." Judge said.

Whitfield Jr was going to get it three times of straight water, this was really going to enhance the show.

"Judge, this little rich bastard is about to do some serious kicking and screaming now in front of the whole world."

We could see the *Medical Examiner Tyince* along with her Team bringing him out *Guarded.*

"Judge...should we have more sympathy for this kid or what?"
I ask.

She said nothing back but this kid believes that because he has money he is more important than anyone else. Laws doesn't pertain to him, giving him the right to whatever he wanted.

"You know I never like this punishment." Judge said.

The cameras zoomed in on the tears from his mom, the *Medic* had given thumbs up, it was that moment we watch him prepared for the worst. I expected him to resist but somehow he didn't as they slid him under this water contraption.

"You know this could result in death easily, if he is not carefully monitored." Judge said.

Medical Examiner Tyince stood near, the thin layer cloth she personally tied around the back of his head, the moment the water made contact with him, He moved slightly, his breathing grew stronger, maybe he was trying to intake as much air as possible. So much silence had come about us, not even the comedians was joking and that was a first. We could see him shaking from fear of what was happening, maybe he thought of death.

"Judge, all that bullshit and arrogance that had been displaying was equal to nothing, no more than a bucket of shit waiting to be thrown out." I said.

We were all about to witness what this little rich bastard was really made of the second when the water touches his ass. We could see the countdown on the monitor…5 4 3 2 1 as the water made its way from the tank into the clear lines. It showered his face, this was easy to watch as you can see his body jerk like if electricity was flowing through him. The more he tried to yell, the more water he had taken in causing him to cough while making one too many crazy sounds that exist between life and death.

"That was really amazing Judge." I said.

Not once in my life, have I ever seen something like that, this man had endured this for 30 seconds and that was just the beginning. *Medical Examiner Tyince* had went to his aid, it took her a few seconds for them to give the thumbs up once again. The sound of him coughing nonstop while trying to catch his breath.

"It was only a small stream Judge." I said.

"When you are suffocation and choking while gasping for air, it feel like a river of water on top of you Mayor." Judge said.

Maybe he was right, the smallest amount has the greatest value knowing Whitfield Jr felt death upon him the entire time. And yet he still denied medical attention but he had been giving the thumbs up once again. It was that moment, there was a malfunction with the machine. The once flowing stream had become like a spray nozzle, it force so much water into Whitfield face that his body wanted to break the straps.

"Judge, I think death was only a seconds away from that little bastard this time."

We watch the cloth being cut away because of knot that had been tied, we watched them place a oxygen masks over his face while trying to calm him down at the same time. It had taken them a moment to get them under control, the protesters became furious and his family was outraged. The second the *Medical Examiner Tyince* had giving the thumbs-up for this to continue, the contraption that had been used before was now being taken away completely due to a malfunction.

"Executioners would've to carry this out." Judge said.

"Wow, really Judge, this disrespecting asshole." I said.

"Yes, Mayor…they are going to have to continue unless he quits or better yet, you pardon him right this second." Judge said.

That wasn't going to happen, it's only 30 seconds or it could be 45 to a minute, im not really sure but at least it not me. That water contraption was programmed to give a few seconds in between the dispersing of the water and now it will be up to the *Executioners* to regulate the time.

"This fool is going to die, they have no love for that idiot, what a good show huh Judge." I said.

We could all see them standing around with large jugs in their hand and others by their side, it wasn't just one that was going to do this. It was all of them at the same time as they cover his body, it appeared to be something out of a horror movie but this was reality. They all move forward until all five of them stood around, the *Medical Examiner Tyince* recheck the dingy looking rag tied around his face. The moment the water rush into him, I could even imagine what he was feeling from the way his body started moving only seconds later. The cameras zoomed in extra close and we could all see that there was no breaks, his entire family stood up looking at the death that shadowed their son.

His mom cried out loud for what was snatched from her crotch, the judge even stood up while the *Medical Examiner Tyince* tried to get to him. She was been forced out by the *Executioners* themselves, this was nothing no more than revenge of the worst kind.

"Judge what a show, everyone is going to remember this forever!" I said.

"It been nearly a minute of straight gushing water into his face nonstop, his own body movement slowed." Judge replied.

The protesters had gotten louder than before causing the *Military* and *Law Enforcement* to react in the worst way.

"Judge, do you think they care that they are being monitored worldwide or do you think they just don't give a shit anymore?" I ask.

She said nothing while looking concern while the *Executioners* emptied gallon after gallon at the same time Whitfield Jr. *Security* had to rush in pulling them away by order of the *Medical Examiner Tyince.* Her entire team rushed in behind her doing what they could, his body became lifeless. Silence existed among some while madness expelled from others.

"Judge this is almost unreal but so amazing at the same time, don't you think?" I shouted.

We watch them work on that little bastard nonstop for several minutes before they had brought him back into this world. *Executioners* stood looking on, they seem so heartless like if they could do it again, they would without remorse.

"Hey, Judge have you ever had a hamburgers and fries from Fred Cafe on the lower side of town." I ask.

She done nothing but look down on me and then back towards Whitfield Jr been given his worthless life back again but I continued asking.

"Judge it's not a real burger unless you taste a little snuff spit, she was one of those real southern dippers and always had a mouthful anytime of the day that you see her." I said laughing afterwards.

"That doesn't even sound healthy." Judge said.

Judge ask me what was funny as I just laugh.

"See, Judge...the wife is the main cook and the southern food isn't that good but the burgers and fries come in a heavily greased stained brown bag. It alone is nothing more than heaven on earth." I explained.

Whitfield Jr had been giving some time to recuperate before being ask if he wanted this to continue, it was my thought that he was without a doubt. This man had dug deep within himself as he wanted this to be over, the sight of the *Medical Examiner Tyince* giving the thumb up that he wanted this to continue. It was that moment, the wheel had been spent.

"Mr. Whitfield Jr you're to be giving 3 flogs to the bottom of both of your feet's and Executioner 5 will be administering the punishment. Is there anything you wish to add or say involving what is about to happen?" Medical Examiner Tyince ask.

Number 5 had gotten up, he stood tall and muscular and his buddies had waved him on, this *Executioner* moved slowly but when he had been giving the go ahead. He swung once to get his distance but the next swing moved Whitfield Jr entire body, it was almost unbearable to watch as the *Medical Examiner Tyince* insisted on checking him. The sight of im barley able to moved.

"Wow, Judge, that little punk is tougher than leather." I said.

It was only minutes later, the *Executioner* had been giving the go ahead, we watch him double his grip as he brought it completely behind him, the crowd roared when they saw a double hitter while the protestor up roared.

"Wow, did you see that Judge?" I shouted.

We watch Whitfield Jr stand up, the oil must to burn like a thousand needles but somehow he ignored the pain as he wobbled on his feet's. He stood in a pocket of his own blood, this fool pushed the sandals away but they had been forced onto him this time. His refusing to sit in the awaiting wheelchair caused him to stumble and bust his mouth when he lost complete control.

"See what ignorance can Judge?" I said.

"Yes I do Mayor but you could've prevented his ignorance from the beginning." Judge said.

What a old bitch, is all I could think, the sight of them doing what they could to stop his bleeding before he had been cleared to receive his next punishment. We could do nothing but watch the wheel been spent once more.

Medical Examiner Tyince had taking the ball.

"Mr. Whitfield Jr you're to receive 4 floggings while the comedians made several jokes from it."

Whitfield Jr had this look in his eyes of anger when they forced him into the sitting contraption from the wheelchair. He made it very difficult for the Guards to strap him down.

"You lucky I wasn't call boy and you better thank your lucky star you little shit but eventually I will be punk!" Giant said.

"That wasn't call for and very unprofessional of him." Judge said.

We watch the *Guards* walk over toward him and forced him to sit back down, the *Medical Examiner Tyince* had giving the go ahead. The sight of Whitefield Jr jerking his hand back with the last strength he had twice.

"Well, Judge...I think Mr. Brave Whitefield Jr has had enough, don't you?" I said.

"Have you had enough Mayor?" Judge said hostily.

Dam whose side is this old b*tch on but I personally don't blame him, the weapon that had been assigned had more leathery strips than I could count.

"Dam, Judge…this Executioner is swinging so hard that when he misses, it's causing him to fall down only to receive medical attention afterward."

Blood covered his darken robe while we listen to the band play to past the time, the only good part was the hoochie dancer. So many big bouncy body parts in school girl's outfits and occasion panty from them flipping around. I myself had several more drinks while Charnel stayed in my ear none stop, she was like a nagging wife about my few sips of liquor. This had become very difficult for me to watch and these few drinks was my only way of being able to stay and endure this awfulness is what I kept telling everyone around me.

"Hey look, he seem to be better now." Judge said.

We watch Whitfield Jr being restrained even more with his palms been placed upright in some horrifying leather looking device. The sight of the *Executioner* now stood directly in front of him ripping him to nothing, his none stop screaming could be heard loudly until it was done. You could see blood dripping while the *Medical Examiner Tyince* done what they could for him but it didn't seem to be enough. The look in his eyes told us that he was done but every time she ask him if he wanted to quit, he yell no loudly. He was going to see this through even if it kill him according to the judge who said she has seen this behavior many times before.

"At least he is almost done, this little bastard is tougher than I would've ever thought Judge." I said.

He sat there in so much pain, if it wasn't for the leather support brace his palms would be hanging lifeless maybe.

"Mr. Whitefield Jr, you are to receive 3 flogging on your upper-lower or center back area, is there anything you like to say or would you like to quit at this time." Medical Examiner Tyince ask.

"No monkey, do your dam job aggressive!" He replied.

Once the she giving the approval, we could see the *Executioner* moving in closer, Whitfield Jr body look so swollen to appoint that the oil seem to have no effect on him whatsoever.

"I really believe that he doesn't care anymore." Judge said.

"That a big man Judge, one hit from him and it was going to be over for Mr. Young Whitfield." I said."

"He is really putting up a good fight, it's obvious that he doesn't want to be in the support brace." Judge said.

We could see them bringing it, Whitfield Jr voice gotten louder along with the cursing that came from his mouth. *Medical Examiner Tyince* had no choice but to inject something to calm him down, we could see his expression change within a few seconds. It had giving him some sort of super life from way he was acting but he had taken all 3 hits. He showed no emotions but sometimes what is done today will be felt tomorrow.

"You are all monkeys, even more so the old black b*itch who made this happen!" Whitfield Jr yell loudly.

That commit was nothing more than aimed at the judge from the way he was now looking directly at her. The protesters cheered him on while the others booed, this went on for several minutes until the *Military* and Law *Enforcement* intervened calming everyone down with painful physical force.

"There will be a 15 to 30 minute intermission." Announcer said.

Whitfield Jr was serious been looked at by the *Medical Examiner Tyince and her Team*, maybe they were trying to figure out why he shown no pain this time.

Chapter 33

Spotlight

"So…Judge, this is your spotlight time huh?" I ask.

She looked at me saying nothing but she knew what I was talking about, this wasn't new for this type of punishment but I was more than surprise that she was going to participate.

"It doesn't matter Judge, you are going to improve the show is what I do know." I said.

Comedians was doing nothing more than making more jokes, it was payback time according to them as I could see the protesters rallying together even closer. Whitfield Jr was fighting from being placed in the wheel chair.

"Look Judge, he still acting a fool." I said.

We couldn't hear what he arguing but I'm sure it was something in the words of how he can walk on his own.

"He leaving a trail of blood Judge." I said.

They had to force him into the wheelchair, it wasn't long after the entertainment that the *Announcer* had call the three girls that he violated and the Officer as well that he has slapped alone with the Judge. They all stood looking at Whitfield Jr return.

"Hey Sheriff, do you think they are going to go thru with it or just leave the past in the past?" I ask.

"Well Mayor, Mr. Whitfield Jr body has been beaten heavily and he is still standing, I believe he is going all the way." Sheriff said.

We watch the *Medical Examiner Tyince* looked him over once more while talking with him.

"Mayor you really going to eat that mix watermelon fruit bowl after adding all that alcohols to it, must be delicious. Sheriff gestured.

There was nothing to do but eat as I looked at the first girl, her name was Sharon Walker, her pinkish outfit made her look all girly with the fattest delicious booty shaking all over the place. It was something that I personally when my hitting repeatedly if the opportunity ever presented itself. She had been ask to spin the wheel but she don't look the type that will go through with it.

"Hey you think she will add that to her pole resume?" Comedian Sam ask.

It was that moment that everyone had gotten a surprise voice, it was Mr. Whitfield Sr on the sound power system.

"This is over and im given $100,000 to each of you who walks away right now."

Sharon was finger by Whitfield Jr as she looked up towards him, the sight of his waited but the angry look in her eyes told the world that he was going to get it and money didn't mean nothing to her. Camera zoomed in on her facial expression as he yell her name.

"Sharon, don't you touch my son, this is over... $250,000 right here and right now." Mr. Whitfield Sr yelled even louder over the sound power system.

Her body movements along with her facial expression had told the world that his money didn't mean nothing to her for what his son did.

"Daddy stop this, don't let this stripper hoe touch me!" Whitfield Jr shouted.

Whitfield Jr was very alert from the way he continue yelling while she swung but did not make contact somehow. We could see her repositioning herself, maybe it was a practice swing as a camera caught tears coming down her eyes. We could see her shaking slightly holding the devil belt.

"Ms. Walker look at me... $575,000 dollars if you stop this now, this is over!" Mr. Whitfield Sr yell loudly.

Sharon looked up at him once more, knowing the money had her thinking, but the pain she felt was deeper along with the horrifying feeling of what she was to live with knowing she had the opportunity to make it right.

"$1 million Miss Walker if you just walk away right now, look at me Sharon...see this check with your name on it!" Mr. Whitfield Sr shouted

We could see tears rolling down her face but there was something about the way she stood made us wonder if she was going to go through with it.

"Sharon look, I just tore up the check and im writing a new one in front of the whole world for $3 million with your name on it, all you got to do is stop right now." Mr. Whitfield Sr shouted even louder.

That moment the sight of her looking up at the monitor that displayed the check was more than what she could handle.

"Drop it stripper whore or your black ass don't get a dime...you hear me daddy, don't give this stripper a dime...now drop it like I said or live the rest of your life been a broke ass black uneducated striper on a pole!" Whitfield Jr shouted to the top of his voice.

She stood there about to cry as tears flowed down her face but the thought of what he just said had come into reality. Or maybe it was the fact that he been through so much, what is one more flogging going to do to him as she looked at him once more and drop the paddle.

"That it, go get that money stripper." Whitfield Jr said while laughing.

Whitfield Sr waited until she gotten directly in front of him.

"I want to see the stripper strip daddy!"

Sharon stood there.

"My son want to see you strip." Mr. Whitfield Sr said.

She stood there about to cry but what was one dance in front of the world, it wasn't like she hasn't done it before.

"Now dance like my son said Ms. Sharon Walker or you get nothing." Mr. Whitefield Sr said loudly.

She had begun moving slowly and dance like if her life had depended on it while removing her cloths until he listening to his son yelling to stop it.

"The other one should be doing the same daddy if she want to get paid as well!" Whitfield Jr shouted.

This had gotten out of control.

"Mayor are you going to allow this to continue and embarrass our country like this?" Judge ask.

I had done nothing but watch the other girl come forward, it was like she didn't give a dam, this woman was about getting paid from the way she started stripping instantly until it had been stop by *Medical Examiner Tyince.* N*ggas went crazy seeing all that chocolate ass bouncing-shaking grinding on each other, even the white protestors cheered none stop. It took the *Military* and *Law Enforcement* to bring order once more before this thing turned into an uncontrollable orgy.

"Wow, I saw that Judge...there is still some freak left inside you huh." I said.

Officer Brashear had been call, this was nothing more than a nightmare for both of these men's but the second he heard the word monkey. It took him into a different world from the anger he had shown...whatever injection he received was making him crazier by the second.

"What are you going to do monkey of the law?" Whitfield Jr yell for the world to hear.

Officer Brashear could cripple this kid easily but the voice he had in his ear from his dad made him hesitate on what he wanted to do.

"$4 million for you to just walk away." Mr. Whitfield Sr yell.

The cameras zoomed in closer on this aging Officer that was now up to 5 ½ to drop it.

"Give this monkey more money, even nappy headed apes can be bought!" Whitfield Jr said loudly.

"This is over!" Mr. Whitfield Sr yelled.

The amount of $6 million was now being offered to him, Officer Brashear was so close to retirement of maybe $20,000 a year if he was lucky. Mr. Whitfield Sr mouth had only gotten louder but Officer Hopkin still had this look in his eyes of revenge and anger. The sight of everyone shouting about his morals of been a peace officer, it was nothing compared to the money being offered.

"You take this money and another half-million if you retire right here on the spot leave that shirt where you stand." Whitfield Sr yelled.

Silence had become of this entire area as he stood there thinking about what was being offered, we see him looking up towards the monitor at this check that had his name on it. All he had to do was be the good little n*gga that Mr. Whitfield Sr wanted as other Officers could be heard yelling in the distance at the sight of one of theirs doing exactly what Mr. Whitfield wanted. The moment he had dropped his gun belt only to witness another Officer had come to claim it.

"Now that dam worthless badge and shirt you if you even want to dime of this money boy! Mr. Whitfield Sr yelled.

We watched him slowly unbuttoned his shirt while another Officer was yelling about pride and integrity while cameras from all over the world zoomed in when he was doing exactly what Mr. Whitfield Sr wanted. I wonder if he thought about how this could be viewed and talked about for years to come all over the world.

"Now monkey boy, you will apologize to my son or your black ass will not get a shiny penny." Mr. Whitfield Sr yelled.

It's amazing, the power money has over peoples.

"On your knees boy just like the rest of them nappy head darkies, you think you are special…get on your knee boy!" Mr. Whitfield Sr yelled.

Protesters cheered like never before, this gave then power while others felt degraded and insulted.

"Sheriff, we see where his useless bastard of a son gets is award winning personality from." I said.

This was nothing more than insanity from what once used to be an honored *Police Officer*, his *Chief* who had made his way toward him. He stood watching, maybe with disbelief of what he was looking at because nothing he said seem to matter.

"Apologize to my son blackie." Whitfield Sr yelled **loudly for the world to hear.**

The *Police Chief Jackson* moved in his path when he saw his *Officer* moving in Whitfield Jr direction but he stood there for a few seconds unknowing what to do.

"Get a move on boy, my patients with your black monkey ass is on thin ice boy!" Mr. Whitfield Sr said.

It was that moment he dropped his head and moved around *Chief Jackson* slowly, this man had no more pride left in him. He had become nothing all for sinful evilness of money in front of the entire world and degrading all that we were as a Nation.

"You will do it on your knees with your head held high monkey, understand me boy!" Mr. Whitfield Sr said.

The world watched him stand there looking down on Whitfield Jr before doing what he was told like a good little plantation house boy.

"Now that a good little obedient buck, now apologized to my son with your head held high boy!" Mr. Whitfield Sr said calmly while grinning to the world.

His voice had been heard throughout the park as he apologize to Whitfield Jr.

"Not come to me personally and get this check boy." Mr. Whitfield Sr said.

It was nothing but a saddest sight to see, not once did he lift his head knowing for the rest of his life that he had been bought and degraded all because of money he never had.

Judge stood looking at what she just saw.

"Hey you, come over and get this check after you apologize to my son just like that other monkeys and you will be on your knees just like the others Judge." Mr. Whitfield Sr. said."

She pick up the pedal that laid near the kid, Mr. Whitfield Sr continue shouting but it had no effect on her. She look at the kid until Mr. Whitfield shouted $9 million.

"Judge you think you are special, you think my money isn't good enough for you, there is no loyalty among any of you monkeys... everyone can be bought even you Judge!"

There wasn't a sound amongst over 50.000 peoples in this park, everyone look on to see what was about to happen.

"Judge look at me when I'm talking to you...ten million dollars, you will take this money and walk away Judge after you apologize to my son!" Mr. Whitfield Sr yelled.

It's amazing, the Judge seem to have the least amount of strength to do any kind of damage and yet she was offered more money than all of them so far. That very second she stop and looked at him before walking toward the *Medical Examiner Tyince* reaching her microphone to speak to the audience. She was giving a really good speech before she went back towards Whitfield Jr to speak directly to him, we couldn't hear what was being said.

"You will not touch my son, looked up at me Judge...look at this...$25 million dollar check on the monitor and all you do is write your name on it. Mr. Whitfield Sr said loudly.

She stood there in silence looking up at the monitor while listening to Mr. Whitfield Sr mouth rambling nonstop. It was that moment out of nowhere the sound of the loudest cry ever heard, it was like the shot heard around the world.

"You'll pay for that Judge...I promise you'll pay for what you just done more than you will ever know, you will pay for the rest of your life...I promise one way or the other Judge, you will pay dearly." Mr. Whitfield Sr yelled none stop.

U.S. Marshall now gathered around the Whitfield's as they watched their son been looked at by *Medical Examiner Tyince and her Team* before he was being taking away by the *Federal Detention Officers*. So much *Security* was needed especially with the Whitfield's if they wanted to get out of here alive. So much hostility was forming before our own eyes, it was like a riot was for sure to take place our *Military* and *Law Enforcement* was now at full alert battle ready.

"I guess the Show is over Chief Jackson." I said.

Nothing good was coming from this, even I was escorted to safety and when it was all said and done over, there was about 300 deaths and over a thousand injuries. It had took about 3 weeks before we could get the city under control from the hatred of what had happen.

Chapter 34

Mr. Whitfield Released

The time had come and I was there, 3 weeks have now passed and Mr. Whitfield Jr had been cleared by *Medical Examiner Tyince and her Team*. This was very unusual to have an entire unit assigned to one person but he was leaving. I had no intentions on going but I was more than happy to see the little bastard leave as I assigned my Vice Mayor to our Deportation Unit to play political exchange. I did take the time to see him being taken from our custody of Liberation as I watched them all drive away.

It only made me laugh knowing he was going to remember this for the rest of his life and not once did that little bastard look my way as if I was even there. I did receive feedback of the U.S. Deportation Officers had taking custody and with all that has happened, it was nothing more than truly amazing how being pull from the right crotch has a major effect on your life. The media had taken interest on Mr. Whitfield Jr release back home and eventually put me in front of the camera as well. So many question had been ask pertaining to his treatment while he was in custody. There wasn't much for me to say but.

"We do have a tough laws but we have a very large population to control and we don't have the money for numerous prisons." 'This nation can afford to house inmates for long, even more so life in prison can't be a part of this country." 'The punishment he had been given sent out a message out to the world that this is not the place to get stupid and expect nothing to happen to you." 'We were no different from any

other country of the world, you will respect our rules and regulations while enjoying yourself at the same time."

That interview had ended as I ended back in my office drinking while Charnel voice had come over the sound system along with another nuisance could be heard.

"Cousin, I got the paper, we made out fat and everybody eats this time."

I looked at him.

"Where is your uniform?" I ask.

He told me how he don't have time for that and he worked out something with the Janitorial Superintendent.

"Meaning what Mr. Bowen's, he is your boss." I said.

"I made him an offer he couldn't refuse in the line of a pine box that he may be living in until judgment day cousin." 'Back to you cousin, you know we made big paper from Whitfield getting his ass beat from vendors the owner, sanitation and every other little grimy deal you had going on." 'You know you put on a good show and I may sure the Executioners got their paper as well cousin." Mr. Bowen said.

"We shouldn't be doing this here…you know that and keep that ghetto shit were it needs to be." I said.

"Cousin don't play me, it's been me has been keeping all hoe houses in check and collecting from all the illegal gambling and operation your moon shine operation operates and keeping them bitches in check you got selling p*ssy for you." 'I don't steal and you get all your paper deposits with that punk ass bank manager that I have to deal with his uppity black ass." Mr. Bowen said.

"Calm down Mr. Bowen's, this isn't the place as I told him thank for all that he does and it doesn't go unappreciated, but you have to learn when to talk and not." I said.

I had told him how he has been shinning too much and he can't be a loud gangsta.

"Too many eyes on you Mr. Bowen's and if we are to make this work, I don't need to have us on some governments list." 'I also need you back in your uniform because you are a struggling worker and get rid of the car you been driving please." I begged.

I had offered him a drink but he had declined telling me how I'm killing myself slowly on that shit.

"Anyway cousin, we've a big shipment coming in from the United States through Mexico and if all goes well, it's a big paper." Mr. Bowen said.

I could do nothing but look at him and ask what shipment because I knew nothing of it but he had told me that everything has been paid off and taking care of.

"Who told you to set this up?" I ask.

He told me how he had taken it up on himself and use all my law enforcement contacts to make it happen, this n*gga hasn't heard a word I've been telling him about how is not all about getting paid. He was nothing more than a loose cannon.

"Cousin you don't have to do nothing but worry about playing politics, you see how I get the job done." Mr. Bowen said.

I had to tell him how the dope has to be a memory of our past and from this moment on, it's over.

"No...you listen to me cousin, nothing is over and your paper will be deposit in three days." Mr. Bowen said loudly.

I watch him leave all I could say was what the f*ck as Charnel walked in.

"Is everything okay?" Charnel ask.

The sight of her made me get frisky but she had taking my hand and slid it under her dress. I pull back instantly, she could do nothing but laugh as I wanted none that bloodiness.

"You would know if he ever taken the time to come and see your son and take care of me sometimes." Charnel said.

I had to get out of here.

"I'll got my cell phone if you need anything, let Ms. Glasco know as well." I said.

"Where you going!" Chanel ask aggressively. "I'm the Mayor...meaning I don't answer to you, you answer to me and with that been said...I'll be back Secretary Charnel."

*"You going to f*ck some nasty b*tch aren't you...you nasty black bastard...f*ck you!" Charnel yelled as I was leaving.*

I said nothing as I ended on the lower side of town with this hoodrat, she had the big booty that was highly needed right about now. Single mom with the fattest monkey I ever seen but the sight of her ghetto ass cousin had arrived just in time to take her little crumb snatcher away. My little man need a fat muscle like her to relieve him while noticing I was getting the evil eye but it didn't matter, hard time and her own struggles may bring her my way for a quick payment when she drops her panties. Good times was on my side more than Hazel cousin, she was giving me an eyes full as soon as the door closed.

I watched that big mother-land bounce like a ragging ocean while she gotten down to her birthday suit, Hazel walk was hypnotic. She was nothing more than eye candy but girls like her was on every corner, this country produced them like rats and roaches not to mention broken down drama filled apartments. Hoodrats are just a touch smarter but she didn't need brains for what I needed her for. There was no need to vacation near some extravagant amusement park, n*ggas like me found all we needed in females like this one with those big soft lips knowing the entry into her kingdom started there.

Hoodrats wasn't all screwed up, they just wanted to be loved anyway possible to help easy their daily battlefield survival. It made them feel stronger knowing they were all weaken maybe from broke childhoods and n*ggas like me filled in where their daddies had been missed. The love she search for would destroy her altogether as I bust deep inside her leaving a few bills hoping it brighten her day like the warm sun when she let me out. I slipped her cousin a bill with my number on it, if I didn't hear feedback from hazel in a negative way than I would hear from her cousin in a positive one in a few days. I ended back at work shortly after relaxing until my door had swung open.

"You visit one of your whorehouses and don't play stupid with me." *Charnel said loudly.*

I said nothing.

"So who is the b*tch?" *'She must be a single mother, what is she 19 or 21 maybe she's 22 or could be 23 maybe with a few kids because this is what you're attracted to!"* *'She knows that you're going to keep breaking her off money as long as she sucks your d*ck or let you f*ck her in every hole she got."* *'Why are you so nasty, why can't one be enough for your nasty ass?"* *Charnel said loudly.*

It was that moment I listening to her speak of my lack of caring. "I'm going home for the day and it didn't even matter if I told her that if she leave, she was fired.

"Go f*ck that bitch you just gotten off of!" Charnel yell.

I could do nothing but watched her leave while taking another drink.

Chapter 35

America

So much has now happen from the Whitfield Jr returned to America, we were at some kind of economic war and we were losing. It eventually had gotten the world big brother attention as America had come to our aide. We were nothing more than there little sister, if imports wouldn't have come our way on a regular basis. We would've destroyed ourselves to almost nothing.

It amazing how one man has the power to cause destruction and more mayhem than what we could handle. Mr. Whitfield Sr mouth never stop running, this man was on every talk show and radio bad mouthing our country. He was making himself becoming more famous than most world known celebrities, the apology he wanted was never going to come his way from us.

This man wanted it heard worldwide but I had no control over our ball-less President who would eventually give him what he wanted. It had only taking me a moment to be call to the Kingdom as I was to travel to Louisiana, it was nothing but a sight to see. This place was built on an old slavery plantation, nothing but the best had been put into it. Anyone who look upon it found it to be very amazing and one day I will be sitting in the top seat.

The life like statues that trailed the half mile stretch of Buffalo Soldiers was very impressive, they line both sides of the path to the Kingdom.

Chapter 36

American President

Upon my arrival, I had been ask to sit at the famous round table, the American President had already been seated along with his Staff as mine followed.

"Gentlemen's im glad to be able to make it but we have major concerns for our country and I will like to thank the American President Obama for taking the time to come this way and help us with our problem." Our, President said.

"Thank you Mr. President." 'America is here to do what we can to help you solve this problem that not just affect you but everyone." American President Obama said.*

I watch both of them go back and for with their appreciation but we need to get to the bottom of this problem.

"I'm going to get straight to appoint, Mr. Whitfield Sr wants a public apology from you Mr. President and your Governor and you as well Mayor, especially you Judge Antione." American President Obama said.

"Okay that is not going to happen as we all know it." I said loudly.

"Mayor, think about what you're saying...think about your economy and economy of this country, peoples are starving from loss of jobs you have rioting in the streets and now you're food supplies are low because nothing is coming in and not to mention how your citizens are protesting." 'Your law enforcement and your military are working nonstop just keep the violence down and I know because we

have imported millions of dollars of medical supplies." 'Vandalism is destroying this country and wherever food you've on your shelves has skyrocketed because this country can't replace stock. American President Obama explained.

"Then why don't you do something about it Mr. President like control those that are making this happen to us." I said

"I'm doing what I can, but I can't control free will of my own citizens that has the power to affect this country from trade." American President Obama said.

That moment I have been told by my own President to basically shut my mouth and how this was mostly my fault.

"You've to understand that Mr. Whitfield Sr is a very powerful man and he is very powerful friends and they can afford to not import a penny into this country." 'They will not be affected financially in anyway shape or form, you must understand what they important to this country is pennies to amount of money they export outside the United States." 'You are at a no-win situation to sum it up and for your country is going to fail in a matter of months." 'You see that I'm trying to do all I can but eventually Congress is going to want more answers, they can make life very difficult for me and the decisions I make regarding this country." 'It will only be a matter time before we may have to place troops all alone our American borders only because this is where your citizens will be heading." American President Obama said.

He was right, history throughout the world has shown that people will search for something better and Mexico is not it. Our own military were probably even flee with their own families leaving us defenseless against millions of angry citizens not to mention our law enforcement.

"So you're telling us to give into Mr. Whitfield." I said.

"I'm telling you to think about your citizens and the destruction of your own cities and your own state and this country." American President Obama said.

"Mayor, if I had to ask you one more time to keep your comments to yourself, I'm going ask you and your Staff to leave. My Commander-in-Chief said.

I can't believe that our own President was going to go along with this, he was so weak and I can't believe this man was even voted into office.

"Mr. Whitfield also wants the release of his family members that you have in custody as well." American President Obama said.

"Um, Mr. President, those two men's broke our rules and regulation and currently at this moment…I'm arranging public punishment and it is my call to decide if I want to give them back sir." I said.

"Mayor…right…if any deal is to be made, it will start with returning his family members back and let's move on from here." American President Obama said calmly.

"Sir, how can you let one man dictate the existence of this country Mr. Commander-in-Chief." I ask.

"Mayor, if you would have done what I ask you to when I came to your city regarding Mr. Whitfield Jr releasing back to his country, none of us would be sitting here right now." 'This is not personal nor is it not about one man, it is about a nation of peoples living together and doing what they can to survive." 'This is nothing more than a nightmare that you started and if it takes me to bow down to this man…I will and so will you and everyone if that's what needed.

"I'm not bowing down to no one sir, not even you." I said.

"Mayor you will do what I ask from this point on and if I knew this was the outcome, I should have relieve you as Mayor on the spot." Commander In Chief said.

"Sir, with all respect you don't have the authority Commander-in-Chief, nor does anyone else here" 'only the citizens have that authority and it takes months to even make it happen sir." I said.

We all sat in silence, not one person has said anything and the Governor himself remain quiet.

"Gentlemen's, I'm glad that you all have a voice but I must reside with your Commander In Chief about what needs to be done and I can only hope, that you all agree with your President." 'You're all fighting a war that you have no possible chance of winning and I'm sure all of you know it." American President Obama said.

I said nothing, neither did anyone else among us all.

"Well, gentlemen's, it's obvious that the decision has been made about what needs to be done." 'So to conclude this discussion, Mr.

Whitfield Sr want this done on the July 4th with world broadcasting following a free party that you're all invited." American President Obama said.*

"This is bull shit." I said.

"Mayor, I'm ordering you to remain silent from this point on and you will do exactly as you are told!" Commander In Chief said.

"Gentlemen's thank you for this opportunity to sit here among you and when I get back to United States I will see that everything goes as normal as I stated." "Thank you for your time your hospitality and God speed be with each of you." American President Obama said.

I watched everyone get up shaken hands like if something great had been accomplished.

"I want to say before we all depart and even more so to you Mr. President of the United State…if we do this… we're nothing more than slaves on America plantation and I now deep down that I'm not the only one who knows that deep inside…even you President Obama." I said loudly.

No one said anything in response before we all departed, I was asked to stay behind to speak with our President. The sight of this man sicken me to my stomach knowing I couldn't wait to get some distance from this coward of a man. I would silence him myself if I had the opportunity but with so much Security, that may never happen.

Chapter 37

The Day

It wasn't long after that meeting Charnel had brought me the paper, those two little bastard made front page news. They had gotten released with no pending charges, maybe even laughing all the way to the United States. What should have been respected was nothing more than a joke, our country was their personal amusement from the beginning to the end.

"Mayor you are aware that the flight to America is tomorrow."
Charnel reminded me.

That next day we departed our country and arrived in the United State and we were to travel once more once we landed. It made no sense but we had to travel the way it was planned, it was nothing more than an insult for what we represented. We had flown in nothing more that look like big yellow banana plane into the city and to make it even worse. They serve nothing but bananas to keep the joke on going as yellow cars awaited us.

Insults had continued, the bars on the outer window represent cages is all we gotten from it but the second we arrive at the hotel. There joking has gone too far especially when we saw nothing but peoples dress as monkeys. The money it took to create this madness could have been spent on making us feel more at home, this was so unprofessional in every way possible. My own Commander In Chief kept his professional bearing the entire time.

The world watch from the many cameras once we land and those that followed, so much humiliation we had to deal with for the next few days and when it was all said and done along with the agreement. The sight of them bringing in costumes had taken this a little too far, it was that moment I watch my own Commander In Chief develop a set of balls before Mr. Whitfield Sr himself. This entire event is made me so angry knowing that money is power and people will do anything for it as that day had ended.

We all stayed up thinking about how Whitfield Sr wanted us to wear monkey costumes and if we didn't, he had actors on standby. It was that moment I just walked away and so did the judge, this has gone too far and there was no way I was going to dress up like a monkey. I said and watch this fool in front of millions of people apologize to both of those bastards, no matter what he believed. It was him that had to live with it, there was still national TV viewed all around the world.

They were all dress like monkeys as me and the judge could do nothing but watch from the conference room knowing everything that this country represented was now nothing more than a world laugh. My own Commander In Chief gave Whitfield Jr diplomatic immunities along with anyone else within his circle. They were all scratching themselves along with everyone else around him during his speech. It wasn't long after that, that we all headed back to our country, what was to be destruction of ourselves have been reversed. Our country had gotten back on track and I gotten re-elected as Mayor while my old friend the Sheriff still had the investigation open and I became his suspect.

Ms. Glasco resigned only to end up working for him, there was nothing I could do to change his way of thinking no matter what I offered him, he should have just closed the case and move on with his life. I still remember that day Charnel had come into my office with the news of his death and his family from a home invasion. They were all murdered and the fire caused them to all have close casket, his young adopted kids was the saddest. I stayed behind for a brief moment saying my goodbye after dropping a flower in each of their graves.

It wasn't long after that, I had come up with financial support from the town folk who mourned for the longest. I broke the ground for each one before leaving the rest for Park and Recreation to finish digging. The sight of 2 adult trees and 3 small tree remain in honor of what the Sheriff stood for in a known local park. It was a place for me people to sit and relax as the tree will grow strong and tall providing shade overlooking Angel

Lake. It wasn't long after that I eventually became Governor of the State for 2 terms serving 6 years.

My cousin Mr. Bowen's was found with numerous bullets to his head, just before my first Presidential election. It was nothing more than an execution styles unsolved murder and closed casket to those that came to pay their respect. I said a few last words after everyone left before dropping a single flower into his grave. Charnel had become my wife before I became President but when it was all said and done. I serving 3 terms or 12 years before I lost to our first woman Commander In Chief, it shock our nation to see it happen so fast. It was an adventure alone with many kids she had giving me.

Mr. Whitfield Jr, his ignorance brought him back to our country on and off for years but one day he never returned back to the United State. He simply disappeared into thin air somehow because till this day it remains an unsolved mystery. My time in office brought change of improving our economy especially with foreign imports although America still play a major part of us. If all fails, we can almost survive without the *World Big Brother.*

We are becoming more independent in this so-call land of monkeys on this plantation that have been given to us. I think of the Judge mostly, she return home only to be forced from the only thing she ever loved doing. Mr. Whitfield Sr made that possible, that day he promise that she would pay dearly and somehow his political power made it happen.

"Make you wonder if she was better off taking the money and leaving like everyone else." I said to myself.

The girls who had been given all that money now live in America, becoming celebrities themselves, Officer Brashear retired and relocated to Santa Monica Ca...he never return back to Africa-America. My life is with my wife Charnel, our kids made us grandparents and this is my story as I grow older each day looking at coastline from my hillside Castle...I had built during my time in the Big Seat.

Declaration of Afro-America Citizenship

We the Peoples of Afro America hold these truths to be self-evident, that all Men's Women and Child are created Equal, that they are endowed by the Creator with certain unalienable Rights that among these are Liberty, Religion, Freedom and the pursuit of Individual Happiness for all Nationalities and Human Existence.

Acceptance of Afro America Citizenship and surrendering your USA birth Citizenship from America.

Yes....._____

No....._____

F*ck No....._____

Your birth name, SS#, home location since birth, Mother n Father financial history alone with their immediate family including yours of past present and estimated future.

President of Afro America

Wayne Anthony Pope Sr.

Political...Drama...Suspense...Horror...Action...Thriller

This story take place before the time of Great Change, so many broken promises since slavery, a new nation is born within America. Revolution of racism and hatred existed before separation that resulted into the largest transformation in America deportation history. Most love country in the world has develop a dark devastation disease of broken political promises with each new leader from one to the next voted into office. This new nation is left to develop themselves from the stone ages as they struggle to maintain from corruption at its highest Government levels.

The son of a billionaire is found guilty of nemourios violations resulting in public punishment. Mr. Whitfield Sr swears to the world that not one hand from that Country of Monkeys will ever touch his son or they will suffer more than any of them know. This one crazy politician that rules the local underworld is becoming a powerful political leader. His deep secrets of psychological demonic insanity goes beyond your own sinful horrifying imagination.

Mayor of Liberation hold the key between both nations becoming at war with each other as America first African President. Has to come up with cure to end this disease curse between the two or sit back and watch their own shadow destroy themselves from within.

"Horrors of the Unknown will always Surface"